A TALE OF HAUNTED APPALACHIA

MOONSHINELAND

RYAN MICHAEL HINES

World Castle Publishing, LLC

Pensacola, Florida

Copyright © 2023 Michael Ryan Hines

Paperback ISBN: 9798891260665

eBook ISBN: 9798891260672

First Edition World Castle Publishing, LLC, October 16, 2023

http://www.worldcastlepublishing.com

Licensing Notes

Cover: Cover Designs by Karen

https://www.cover-designs-by-karen.com

Editor: Karen Fuller

AUTHOR'S NOTE

Dear Reader,

This is Moonshineland, a story of Haunted Appalachia.

Based on Horace Kephart's true account of moonshine, murder, and mountain mayhem "Our Southern Highlanders" and Madeline Vinton Dahlgren's classic description of the Appalachian occult "South-Mountain Magic," Moonshineland is the story of my attempt to discover the truth behind a Prohibition-era manhunt for a fugitive Moonshiner.

But instead of uncovering the story of a human criminal, I found evidence of an ancient Appalachian Evil that has been hiding in the hills for centuries. And this ancient Evil was not happy to have been disturbed. Read on if you dare.

Yours,

Armandine

PROLOGUE

It was dark in that deserted Appalachian mountain town. Not late, just wintertime dark.

It should have been cold, but warm weather was hanging on. Indian Summer. That's what my adoptive father used to call it. He died in 2000, over twenty years ago. Strange of me to think of him now, but memories are always strange.

Wind was blowing the last autumn leaves across the old brick sidewalk, but the air felt almost hot on my face. And I was alone. Alone when it found me. Something I could not believe was real.

I heard it before I saw it. A slow, deep, growl.

I didn't look back. Not at first. I was, I was too afraid to look, you know what I mean? Maybe afraid is the wrong word. Yeah, not afraid. Unable, unwilling. I was *unwilling* to admit what I was feeling was real. So I just kept walking, moving down the small main street and praying that I would find the address written on the scrap of paper I had clutched in my hand.

13 B North Market Street.

But the growling got louder. *Closer.*

I could feel my breath wheezing, catching in my throat. I kept looking for the address, but every door was shut, and all the lights were out. I couldn't find 13 B to save my soul.

Then, the growl behind me changed. Its pitch rose, morphing from a guttural rumble to a God-awful, murderous howl.

That noise, that howl... It sounded like...it sounded like the last thing you hear before you're taken. It was as if the end of everything was right behind me.

So I decided I had better quit walking and start running.

Without looking back, I just ran. But it wasn't behind me. Not anymore.

Lightning struck. I heard the howl again and saw something lurking in the dusk.

I didn't get a good look. It was so dark. But when the lightning...I thought it was in front of me. Head low, mouth open, black fur standing up on the ridge of its back, rippling as waves of rage danced under its skin. I knew it was here to take me. I was going to die. And then the sky just opened up, and I heard a voice as rain began to fall.

"In here," the voice said.

I looked over and saw an arm outstretched from an open shop door. I could have sworn that moments ago, there was nothing there but some crumbling brick facade, but I was so freaked out by the thing chasing me through the dark that I decided to take my chances. I've always been a bit of a gambler.

So I grabbed ahold of the stranger's hand, intertwined my fingers in theirs, and hoped for the best.

PART I
THE ARRIVAL OF THE SNAKE STICK MAN

I heard an old-fashioned doorbell ding as I stumbled through the threshold and into the small mountain bookshop. The storm was raging outside, rain slapping on the glass door, thunder rumbling in the distance. I was just able to make out the address written above the shop entrance. 13 B North Market Street. But that was impossible. I had been running for a long time. I had taken a lot of random turns down random streets and was pretty sure I wasn't even on Market anymore when the hand appeared and helped me inside.

I looked at the man standing in front of me, the owner of the hand that had pulled me in. He was old. Long hair and a gray beard that reached all the way down the front of his faded flannel shirt. As I stared at him, I realized I was shaking and tried unsuccessfully to stop myself. I wondered if it was the cold rain on this otherwise warm day that was giving me the shivers.

The man moved past me and locked the door. He peered out through the glass into the storm. I wasn't sure, but he looked like he might be afraid. Not as freaked out as me, a stranger in a strange town, shivering from shock and thinking I might just have hallucinated some sort of, of I don't even know what. But still, a little afraid.

Maybe he was looking for what had chased me here. But that couldn't be. What I saw wasn't real. Just my mind playing tricks. Had to be. Then I realized he was waiting for flashes of lightning and counting silently to himself until the thunderclap rolled over the hills.

"One...two...three..." he murmured under his breath between each flash of lightning and rumble of thunder.

"Are you the Bookseller?" I asked him. He didn't verbally respond to my question. Just nodded slowly, still staring out the window and silently counting the seconds between the lightning and the thunder.

"Getting closer," he whispered.

I didn't understand. He wasn't making a lot of sense. None of this was making a lot of sense.

"What is?" I asked. "What is getting closer?"

Again, the Bookseller did not respond to my question or to me. It was almost like he didn't even see me there, which was starting to piss me off. So I raised my voice.

"Why did you let me in here?"

And just like that, the Bookseller turned, brushed past me again, and went to the counter. He had an old-fashioned cash register, the metal kind with a bell that rings when you punch in the prices. Must have been antique. As a matter of fact, everything in the low-ceilinged shop looked at least a hundred years old. Even the air smelled ancient. Anyway, there was a book sitting by the register. He picked it up and extended it toward me.

"This is it, isn't it?" he said.

I looked at the manuscript in his hand but did not immediately recognize it. "This is what?" I asked.

"The book. The book you were interested in." He was looking straight at me, face more animated than before. No question about whether or not he saw me now.

"Your name is Armandine, yes?" he continued. "You are the woman who contacted me."

He was right. I don't know how he could be so sure who I was, but yes, I was named Armandine, and I had called a few weeks ago and contacted him about a book. I just wasn't sure that it was this book, the one he was holding.

I should probably stop here and tell you a little bit about me and why I was here in this tiny

Appalachian town in the first place. I'm a reporter. I work for one of the last small town papers left in the Eastern mountains, and we were doing a puff piece on famous residents of the local area. The story was hopefully going to create public interest, attract tourism, and boost the local economy. However, not many current mountain natives were well known, or known at all, really, so the story was beginning to focus more on former residents than current ones.

My research had turned me on to an author who had lived in the mountains back in the 1920s. Further research had uncovered something strange about this author's life, his work, and his death. Something about a lost manuscript, illegal activity, and even, possibly, murder.

My editor wasn't interested. My "hundred-year-old hunch," as he put it, didn't paint the locals in a positive light. So he told me to drop it and stick to the softer human interest angle. But you'll figure this out about me sooner or later, so I'll just tell you now. I'm hardheaded, especially when I have already made up my mind, which, in this case, I had. So, despite what my editor wanted, I started searching for this author's lost manuscript, even though I was reasonably sure my editor was right, and it didn't exist. Still, I ran down a lead that brought me here to this little bookshop deep in the mountains and put me across the room from this strange, old bookseller.

I took the book out of his hand and looked it over, then asked what felt to me like a more pressing question than anything to do with antique literature. "Why did you lock the door behind me?"

He didn't answer, just pointed at the book I now held.

"That's the one," he said. "The rare second edition pulled by the publisher in 1922. The one you asked about. The lost edition."

It wasn't a question. The Bookseller was sure he had spoken to me and that this was the book I had asked him about. But none of that made sense. Things felt...wrong somehow. The location of the shop, or rather my inability to locate the shop, the...thing that I thought I had seen outside.

I decided to confront him. "I've been looking for your shop all day, but I couldn't find it. I looked up the address on Google Maps, Waze, Yelp, everything. No luck. I even drove to the next two towns and tried to find their 13 B North Market Streets in case I copied down the wrong address. But still nothing. So I drove back here, to this town. And then I'm walking all over this afternoon, up and down North Market, and I can't find 13 B anyplace. But as soon as the storm rolls in and that stray dog—"

"Weren't no stray dog," the Bookseller

interrupted.

I decided to ignore that last statement and keep talking.

"As soon as whatever it was that scared me... when I start running...I mean, I'm not even on the right street anymore. But you reach out from nowhere and pull me in here, a place I didn't see before. And it's 13 B North Market? How is that even possible?"

Again, he just sort of looked at me before nodding slowly and going back to the door. As he turned, I could hear him say something quietly.

I think he said, "My shop's here when you need it."

He was counting the seconds between the lightning and thunder again. There wasn't much time between anymore. "Storm's on top of us now," he said, "Better wait it out here. You can read that book while the weather passes."

"I'm not sure that's such a good idea," I said. The Bookseller took a deep breath.

"It explains it," he said.

I was lost. "Explains what?"

He smiled at me for the first time, and only then did I realize how frightening he was when he wasn't smiling. He was not menacing. Not on purpose, anyway. But he was frightening. The man looked like an eternity. Like you could fall into him the way light falls into a black hole and just keep falling, forever until eventually your atoms pulled apart from each other, and you weren't anything anymore.

His face was stone serious as he spoke the following words to me. "It explains what chased you here. What is waiting outside that door for you if you leave."

Now, I know what you are thinking. I was thinking it, too. But for some reason, a reason I still cannot fully explain, I didn't leave. Instead, I took the book out of his hand and sat down on an old couch in the front of the store. The couch faced the big front window and an old TV set. It was the kind of set up mountain shops used to have back in the day when neighbors would head down to the General Store to have a drink of 'shine and watch the one television in town together.

The book cover was faded, but the title was clear enough. *Our Southern Highlanders. A Narrative of Adventure in the Southern Appalachians and a Study of Life Among the Mountaineers.*

I opened the cover and read the handwritten notes at the top of the first page. "What follows are the events, true to a word, that my publisher refused to allow in the manuscript on account of them being considered 'Too fantastical to be believed' and 'of a superstitious and satanic nature, obviously untrue and unfit for publication.' But what follows is most definitely true. I saw it with my own eyes." The note was signed, Horace Kephart.

That was the name of the author I was researching.

"Well, go on then," the Bookseller encouraged me, "Read it. This is what you were looking for, wasn't it?"

It was. It was exactly what I had been looking for. The rumored lost manuscript for *Our Southern Highlanders*, a book about Appalachian culture Kephart had written in the 1920s. The official version contained stories about moonshiners and the lawmen who hunted them. It is widely available since it has passed into the public domain. You can google it and download a free pdf. It's that easy.

But I wasn't looking for the official version, the one that contained prose sanitized by editors and publishers. I was looking for the lost edition, the one that was rumored to contain first-hand accounts of supernatural activity in the Appalachian mountains. However, a big part of me never believed the lost second edition existed.

Like the black-haired thing that had chased me into the Bookseller's shop, Kephart's lost manuscript was something I wondered about but didn't really believe actually existed.

"Yet, it does," said the Bookseller, answering my unasked question like he could read my mind.

I shook off the dread I was feeling, turned the page, and, against my better judgement, started to read the lost manuscript.

The first page began —

CHAPTER 1

WHITE LIGHTNIN', BLACK MAGIC.

When I was a child, my mother told me; if you have faith the size of a mustard seed, God will smile on you, and you will be saved. I was little then and did not understand. So I asked her, what does God want me to have faith in? She just laughed and said, "You are a different sort of child, ain't you, Horace?"

Well, I never did have much faith, but I wanted to. So, I did my best to believe when I could. I believed in love, and it broke my heart. And I believed in what the Bible taught me, that there is evil out there in the darkness, and that very nearly cost me my soul.

You must know, dear reader, I have always been a wanderer. If I had a bedroll, a hatchet, some cartridges, and a gun, I found I could go most anywhere and do most anything I needed and everything I wanted. Life in the wild was all I ever desired until, after one lonely night too many huddled alone in the dark, I took a few years off from my mountain travels to finish my education, marry a woman, and father a child.

There are precious few things in this life they cannot take away from you. An education is one, but a family is not. Mine left me not long after my thirtieth birthday. And so to wandering in the Appalachian wilderness, I returned. I came finally to live in Bryson City, the county seat of the same county in which I had first appeared as a resident of the mountains.

To call it a city is to overstate things a bit. A stretch of dirt road, a general store, and a hotel that was, in truth, more a bar room in which drunk men slept was all that separated Bryson City from the hills and hollers that surrounded it.

The land itself was overrun with moonshine and the folk who made it. A self-reliant group, they were good with a rifle and master hunters of animals and, sometimes, men. I found myself drawn to these rugged mountain people who brewed white lightning in the woods and outran Revenue men on treacherous mountain roads.

It was along in October of 1922, I believe, that a sturdy, dark-eyed stranger came to the old hotel where I lived and was introduced to the landlord, a young woman called Rose, by the Indian Agent from Lufty, who had brought him over in his car. I remember the time of year because the trees had mostly lost their leaves, but the weather was oddly hot. Indian Summer, I think they say. That's what my father used to call it, anyhow.

The Indian Agent was thoroughly rattled from the drive over, having almost lost control of the car at the hairpin turn at the end of Grayson's Gap, just outside town. But as for the Stranger, he was not rattled at all. As a matter of fact, he was, if anything, unnervingly sanguine.

He wore a big cowboy hat, Lucchese boots, and two Luger semi-auto pistols in shoulder holsters under his black oilskin coat. He was obviously not from around here. Everyone assumed from his bearing and dress that he must be from the West. And even though he wore his guns under his coat, it was obvious to every Mountain Man and Woman that he wanted it known that he was carrying.

But the thing that caused the most stir as he sauntered into the saloon where I sat reading, more than his strange dress and German pistols, was his walking stick.

Made from a gnarled oak branch, it was as tall as he was. Over six foot, a hand-carved serpent wrapped around the length of it, a real snake's rattle near the bottom that vibrated with each step, and a carved mouth, open, fangs extended in an unending hiss, at the top, next to the Stranger's head.

And I swear to you, as the Stranger stood in the doorway, backlit by the sun, the serpent on his walking stick *moved*.

It turned its head and stole a glance at me.

I looked around the room at the other men inside to see if they had caught sight of this strange and miraculous incident. But none of the mountaineers, clad in their faded denim overalls, chewing their tobacco, and drinking their illicit spirits, seemed to have noticed anything strange about the wooden snake. They only had eyes for the man who carried it. And they did not like this stranger much. They liked him even less when he opened his mouth and spoke.

"I am looking for Buck Ruff," he said. "And I know, despite your inevitable protestations to the contrary, all of you could tell me where he's hiding and that before the sun sets tonight, one of you will."

Now, Buck Ruff was a notorious local moonshiner. He, his brother and their daddy had been making 'shine and running it across state lines for years without any real trouble from the Revenue Men. The law had only come down on them when they started smuggling it across the Qualla Boundary into the nearby Cherokee Reservation.

Apparently, the Federal Government felt it was the only organization that should be allowed to interfere with the sovereign Cherokee Nation and took offense at the Ruff family muscling in on what had been, up until that point, a strictly Federal racket. So Buck had been arrested by a Federal Marshal and locked up in the local jailhouse.

But ol' Buck didn't cotton to that prison cell at all.

So the night they locked him up, and this is true, mind you, he ripped the metal bed frame in his cell apart, used a piece of it to knock a hole in the brick wall, tore and tied his bedclothes into a rope, and climbed down from his second story cell to the ground below. As you can imagine, this created quite a ruckus, and the Marshal that had arrested ol' Buck was waiting for him when his feet touched mother earth. But Buck didn't let that stop him.

He snapped that Marshal's neck with his bare hands like a child snapping a twig and took off into the night. There was outrage the next morning amongst the federal lawmen, and a huge manhunt was organized, but to no avail.

They must have sent a hundred men into those hills and two hundred dogs. But every bloodhound they sent out to hunt Buck down either turned coward and run home or met with a violent end.

But nobody ever saw what killed those dogs. Not a one, and there had been dozens torn apart. Some said it was bears or coyotes or panthers that did it. But again, there were dozens of mutilated hounds, but not a single wild animal was sighted during the entire manhunt. It was as if all the predators of the mountains had hid away, like they were as afraid of whatever was lurking up there as the bloodhounds were. After a week's time, enthusiasm and resources for the search dwindled. Most of the Marshals went home, and Buck Ruff was lost to the hollers and hills.

Buck had been on the run for the better part of two years now. The law had had no luck catching up with him and appeared unable ever to do so. A fact, it now appeared, that this Stranger dressed in black, with the Luger pistols tucked under his arms and the sinister Snake Stick in his right hand, was about to try and change.

A big man in the back of the room, I think his name was Hol, stepped forward, wiped tobacco spit from his beard, and looked the Stranger in the doorway up and down.

"Who wants to know where Ol' Buck Ruff be hidin'?" he growled.

"I do," said the Stranger in the doorway, "and I'd appreciate it if you would tell me quickly. I am a busy man of work, not a day-drinking man of leisure as you appear to be."

Well, I am not sure if Hol knew, exactly, what a man of leisure was or that he had just been insulted, but one thing he knew for sure. He did not like the Stranger one gol' darned bit.

"You fast with them pistols, Snake Stick Man?" he asked. The Snake Stick Man nodded. Hol hitched his own gunbelt up around his waist and spat more tobacco juice. "Let's see how fast," he said.

"Not in my place!" Rose, the local hotelier and owner of this fine establishment, yelled from behind the bar, "You two wanna act foolish? You act foolish outside," she commanded.

And so they did.

***

We gathered outside the Hotel, anxiously awaiting the commencement of the quick draw competition between the large Mountain Man named Hol and the stranger dressed in black, The Snake Stick Man.

Hol squared off on his side of the street and waited impatiently as The Snake Stick Man took his time getting ready, checking the rounds in his pistols and adjusting his holsters. Finally, Hol lost his patience and hollered to The Snake Stick Man, "Hellfire! For a busy feller in a hurry, you sure dally. Are you a man, and we got-damned gonna do this now? Or are you a yellow coward, and we are not?"

But The Snake Stick Man still seemed to be in no rush. He stood there, leaning against his serpentine walking stick. He cocked his head, listening for something we could not hear.

"All in good time. All in good time," was his only response, and that enraged Hol even further.

As we waited for the trouble to begin in earnest, my friend Glenn Owl sidled up to me. Glenn was tall and tan, a Cherokee born and raised behind the Qualla Boundary. He had two deep scars on each palm stretching from his fingertips to his wrists that he earned across the sea somewhere in the trenches of that European cataclysm. You see, when the Great War commenced, Glenn had immediately volunteered.

He was sent across the ocean and conducted himself well in that savage spasm of violence. On one particularly grim day, the Huns made a charge across No Man's Land and came into Glenn's trench at the precise time he and his best wartime friend, a young local of French extraction named Felipe, had run out of ammunition. As a large Hun drove his bayonet home toward Felipe's heart, Glenn grabbed the blade with bare hands, ignored the pain and blood as it filleted his skin, pulled the rifle out of the Hun's grip, and proceeded to beat the exasperated German to death with it.

Felipe was so grateful that he subsequently introduced Glenn to his younger sister, which is how my Cherokee friend came to return home to the Appalachian mountains with two large scars, one small

French wife, and a tiny toddler son. The story of how Glenn "caught" the German bayonet and "caught up" with the French woman gave rise to Glenn's nickname, "Catch," which was better known to everyone in Bryson City than his true name ever was.

When I first came to Bryson City, I was regarded as a stranger, an outlander. Catch and his family were the only friends I made for some months. I shared many meals at his table and enjoyed his family's company for a long time before I felt truly accepted here. My time in Catch's home allowed me to forget, for a moment at least, the searing loneliness I had felt ever since my wife and child left me.

Although, when I saw Catch with his son and saw how much they loved each other and enjoyed each other's company, a different kind of loneliness struck me. It was hard to see a man so in love with his family be able to spend time with them when I was not.

Even so, the love Catch had for his wife and son warmed my heart and gave me hope for the world.

Anyway, as I said, Catch sidled up next to me, his little son in tow, and asked what was going on. As I explained the situation to him, a strange thing happened. Hol was getting so impatient that he was preparing to draw down on The Snake Stick Man despite the stranger's direction to wait when we all finally heard what The Snake Stick Man had been listening for all along.

There was something moving in the brush.

A mountain Rattler slithered out from the brush on the side of the road and headed straight toward The Snake Stick Man. "The hell is this?" Hol mumbled, but he lowered his gun anyway.

The Mountain Rattler coiled itself up inches from The Snake Stick Man and prepared to strike.

Far from showing signs of fear, The Snake Stick Man looked calm. He stared into the Rattlesnake's eyes with an expression, not unlike a lover's unspoken request and did not move except to set down his walking stick and crack his knuckles and the serpent *hissed* and *spat*.

"By god!" Hol yelled, his rage at the dark Stranger completely transformed into concern, "Yon serpent will make a corpse of you, man! Get you away!"

Catch and his son were similarly entranced by the dramatic showdown between man and beast, especially the boy.

And then, just as we were all sure it would, the snake struck out!

But, with God as my witness, as the snake opened its jaw and lunged, fangs dripping with black blood poison, only inches away from the Stranger's flesh, it was blown to bits by his Luger pistols, which cleared leather, took aim at hip level, and fired with a speed and accuracy I not only had never seen in all my travels in all my days but that I did not believe possible. As a matter of fact, had I not seen The Snake Stick Man's skill with the weapons myself, I would never have believed it to be within the realm of physical possibility.

Needless to say, Hol, having witnessed this display of firearm proficiency as well as The Snake Stick Man's apparent ability to commune with serpents, decided a duel was unnecessary at best and suicidal at worst. Hol shook his head and raised his hands in surrender as The Snake Stick Man holstered his pistols. The Snake Stick Man waved his hand in acknowledgment of Hol's capitulation, and Hol visibly relaxed. He approached The Snake Stick Man and mumbled something under his breath.

"What was that, friend?" The Snake Stick Man asked.

"The Sugarlands," Hol repeated, "They say Buck, and mebbe his kin too, are hid out in the Sugarlands."

The Snake Stick Man nodded in thanks and stooped to retrieve his walking stick.

The small crowd that gathered to watch the showdown between Hol and the Stranger had already dispersed save Catch, his boy, and myself, who had, for some unspoken reason, all three decided to hang back, so no one but us witnessed the following event. As we finally turned to go back into the hotel, Catch's son grabbed his father's hand and pointed back at The Snake Stick Man, who was crouched down low. He held the walking stick in one hand and waved his other over the deceased mountain rattler.

"Look, Papa!" the child exclaimed.

I hesitate to relate to you the following, as I fear you may find it blasphemous. But it cannot be blasphemy to write the truth, can it? If you believe it is, I suggest you read no further.

Now, as The Snake Stick Man waved his left hand, the carved walking stick in his right transformed into a moving, breathing serpent, just like the rod of Moses did in the book of Exodus. It dropped to the ground, coiled itself around the broken body of the mountain rattler, and hissed.

And, as The Snake Stick Man's serpent uncoiled itself from the body of the dead mountain rattler, the formerly deceased serpent returned to life and slithered away into the brush. And as it did, the walking stick returned to the Stranger's hand, stretched out straight, and became carved wood again. Once its transformation back to an inert form was complete, The Snake Stick Man stood up, looked us dead in the eyes, and smiled.

"Did you see that Catch? Miraculous!" I

exclaimed.

"Nothing but a cheap magic trick," Catch retorted. Catch had seen many a charlatan Gypsy's magic show while he was in Europe, and his wartime experiences had turned him into an avowed atheist besides. I, on the other hand, was searching these mountains for answers to big questions and thought perhaps I had found some in this strange man dressed all in black.

The Snake Stick Man then approached us. Catch stood up straight and put his son behind him. I unconsciously let my hand drop down toward the pistol I kept at my side. Despite my curiosity, the man made me nervous.

"Friends," The Snake Stick Man purred, smiling again, "No need to be afraid. I mean you no harm. As a matter of fact, I am the bearer of good news." As The Snake Stick Man spoke, he noticed that Catch's son was staring at his carved walking stick.

"Shall I make one for you, boy?" The Snake Stick Man asked. The child nodded vigorously, and The Snake Stick Man picked a suitable piece of wood up from the ground, sat down beside the road, and began carving with the knife he kept in his belt.

"As I said, I have good news." The Snake Stick Man whittled with remarkable skill and speed as he spoke to me and my Cherokee friend. "Horace Kephart and Catch, is it? We three are going on a raid into the Sugarlands after Buck Ruff. Tonight."

Catch recoiled at the sound of his nickname. "How do you know who we are?" he demanded. The Snake Stick Man smiled that charming smile again. "No need to worry. I am a United States Marshal, and I have been sent by an exasperated United States government to track down and apprehend Buck Ruff and bring him to justice. But I cannot do it alone and am in need of deputies. So, I will be deputizing you two. We head out tonight."

I was quite taken aback and could not find my words, but Catch had no such problem. He spit and shook his head. "Why would we go anywhere with you?"

Again, The Snake Stick Man smiled.

He had finished carving the stick and handed it to Catch's son, who took ahold of it with the kind of reverence only a small child is capable of.

"I have done my research, boys," The Snake Stick Man continued, "and here is the situation. I cannot trust these local fellows. They are moonshiners to a man and will not give up the location of Ruff willingly and may even offer me help only to lure me into the Sugarlands to dispatch me there. But you two are outsiders. You, Kephart, are a stranger here doing his best to fit in as you struggle to make ends meet.

Your publisher is getting frustrated with you, is he not?"

It was true. I financed my freewheeling mountain lifestyle by writing articles for hunting magazines and the occasional book on mountain men and their ways. But lately, I had had little luck with my prose, and my wallet was not only empty, it was inside out. I was incurring debts in order to procure the bare necessities of life. In short, I needed a story to write, and I needed it now.

"Well," The Snake Stick Man continued, "a manhunt into the wilderness should give your publisher exactly what they want. And you, Catch," The Snake Stick Man turned to face my friend. "You need the five hundred dollars bail money back, don't you?"

Since returning from the war, Catch had made his living as a Bondsman and Bounty Hunter. He had posted bond for Buck Ruff and lost a considerable sum when the man had escaped. It was a crippling financial blow he and his family had not recovered from. I know Catch needed the money. His frayed coat and his son's threadbare clothing were a physical reminder of the existential threat poverty posed to all of the people living in the mountains.

The Snake Stick Man stood, looked us over again, and leaned against his serpentine walking stick.

"Say nothing now. I will be at the edge of town tonight, after sundown, where the two roads cross. If you are there, I will know you aim to help me in my mission and that I have made two new friends. If not, then I know you plan not to aid but perhaps to interfere with my investigation and that I have possibly made two new enemies in this wilderness. I sincerely hope that is not the case. See you tonight."

The Snake Stick Man moved to leave us, then stopped and turned around. "Oh, and I trust you can provide your own horses. There are no roads where we are going."

CHAPTER 2
A RAID INTO THE SUGARLANDS.

A cool breeze cut the humid Indian Summer air that night, alarming the chirping crickets and promising a change in the weather.

I saw an old Woman relaxing on her front porch, watching the road out of town. She sat in a handmade bentwood rocker and moved slowly back and forth in the dark, her craggy face barely visible, illuminated by an orange glow each time she took a puff off her corncob pipe. She spoke to me as I rode past her, mounted on a borrowed horse.

"Comin' up a storm this night, Horace. You headed into the Sugarlands?"

I nodded. Yes, I was headed into the Sugarlands.

"Watch you for trouble," she warned.

I do not think she was speaking about the weather.

I found Catch afoot just outside of town, leaning

against his good Jack mule, saddle laying on the ground beside him. He was smoking a hand-rolled cigarette. Catch hardly ever smoked anymore, only when he was greatly troubled. And I had seldom seen him so distressed. The Great War had evened him out, taken off the edges. After the horror of the trenches and the bayonet that scarred his hands, it took quite a lot to rattle him.

As a matter of fact, I had only one other time seen the man with a cigarette in his mouth, and that had been the night, perhaps a year ago, that his wife miscarried their second child. He still had her blood on his hands when I saw him strike a match. He had been so unsteady that night I had to light his tobacco for him.

"Well," I offered, perched in my saddle, "I've heard it's easier on the legs during a long journey to ride one's mule than walk in front of it, carrying the saddle yourself."

Catch took one last, deep pull off his cigarette, then tossed it away. "Don't plan to mount up unless I decide to go with you and The Snake Stick Man. And I have not yet made up my mind," he grunted.

Just then, an owl hooted. I shook my head at the sound.

"A bad omen, that," I muttered.

Catch looked up at me. He was angry.

"To hell with omens, Horace. You think I'm a superstitious man? Why? Because I am Cherokee? Because of the mountains where I was born?"

"No, Catch," I said, "I think I am a superstitious man. And these mountain people have done little to dissuade me of the notion. Forgive me. I did not mean to insult you."

Catch rolled his shoulders, patted his mule, and seemed to settle a bit. "I don't like it," he said, "this Marshal makes me nervous."

"Is it the magic that bothers you?" I asked.

Catch just shook his head, no. "There is no such thing as magic, Kephart. Only tricks. And I have trouble trusting a man who likes so much to play tricks."

"Then stay home, Catch. Stay with your family, and I'll go alone with him. The Snake Stick Man was right when he spoke to me today. I need to sell a story, or my time in the wilderness will come to a close."

At these words, my friend Catch began to look upset again. He rolled another cigarette and lit it.

"Bullshit, Horace," he spat, "You could use the money, but you don't need it. You're as capable a mountaineer as any white man I ever met. If you want to stay in these mountains, you'll stay. There's enough game to keep you a hundred winters and enough land to hide out in for ten lifetimes. Or you could just stay with me and my family. You know you are always welcome. It isn't for want of money that you are out here a-horseback in the dark."

Catch took a long draw off his cigarette and pointed at me, his dark eyes piercing the night.

"You *want* to go."

I watched Catch smoke and thought about what he had just said to me.

It was true. I did want to go. I could not say why, but there was something drawing me to this Snake Stick Man, something pulling me out into the deep wilderness onto this manhunt. And I could not for the life of me say what it was. True, I needed money, but Catch was right. I could do without it. What I could not do was walk away from the chance to learn more about the man who could shoot like a god and raise snakes from the dead.

"Stay, Catch. Stay with your wife and son," I said.

But even as I spoke, Catch was swinging his saddle up onto the Jack mule's back and tightening the cinch. He flicked his second cigarette away, gathered his reins, and stepped up into the saddle.

"You may be able to live without money, Kephart," Catch grumbled, "but I can't. If I don't get that five hundred back, I am damn sure my wife will leave me. She'll put up with a lot, but not poverty. I need that bail money returned. And I won't lose my family because I am afraid to ride into the mountains with some dark stranger."

***

We found The Snake Stick Man right where he said he would be, waiting at the crossroads in the dark, mounted on a bright white mare. He was smiling that great, charming smile of his.

"Good. Good!" he said as we approached.

"When this is done, justice will be served upon the Ruff family, your future secured Kephart, and your bail money returned to you, Catch. I hope you boys brought coats. I believe the weather is about to turn."

And with that, The Snake Stick Man turned his white mare and rode off into the darkness with us in tow. "We ride through the night, boys, and will stop for provisions in the valley first thing tomorrow."

But we did not make a full night's ride. Only an hour or so later, we found ourselves pinned down by a raging thunderstorm and took refuge in a small mountainside cave, leaving the horses loose under a grove of trees.

I was counting the time between lightning strikes and the thunder they caused, hoping in vain to discover that the storm was moving away from us as Catch struggled to roll a cigarette out of very damp makings.

That's when we heard it. A blood-curdling,

bone-chilling howl.

"You have wolves yet alive in this part of the country?" The Snake Stick Man asked us, apparently genuinely surprised.

Catch ignored the question and only opened his mouth to curse his soaking wet tobacco, leaving me to answer.

I shook my head. "No," I told The Snake Stick Man, "the last one was shot dead in 1887." The Snake Stick Man smiled, not as charming a smile this time.

"Then what was that?" The Snake Stick Man demanded as another howl echoed across the mountain.

I found that I had no good answer for the man.

We spent a sleepless night huddled in our cave and ventured out with the sun the next morning, eyes bloodshot from exhaustion and ears ringing from thunderclaps. It was cold, the storm having chased off the unseasonably warm temperatures, but we were so glad the rain was over we did not care about the chill. Our relief was short-lived, however.

Catch saw them first, I second.

The two horses and Catch's one good mule lay dead on the ground, their throats torn out and stomachs laid open.

"My God," I gasped, "what could have done this?"

Catch whistled and pointed at the ground. "Here, Kephart," he said, "On the ground. Headed away from us."

My eyes followed Catch's hand, and I saw them. The tracks of a huge animal, some sort of canine, I was sure, circling the dead equids and then heading away, over the mountain and toward the valley.

"That's not the worst of it, boys," I heard The Snake Stick Man say. He had doubled back the way we rode in and was pointing at a set of the same tracks that came up the mountain trail behind us.

"Christ," Catch muttered under his breath as he rolled a cigarette, "it was following us. Whatever did this, it was behind us all night."

Catch's conclusion made The Snake Stick Man smile again. "Yes, boys. It appears the hunters may have become the hunted."

"What does that mean?" I asked. Catch would have asked the same question, but he was too angry to speak. The Snake Stick Man leaned against his staff and cocked his head.

"I'll tell you on the way," he said.

"On the way where?" Catch demanded, finally finding his voice.

"We'll walk over the mountain and into the valley, boys," The Snake Stick Man commanded, "and on the way, I'll tell you what I should have told you before we left. There is more to Buck Ruff's story than I have led you to believe."

And with that, The Snake Stick Man started walking. Catch looked around at the destruction lying on the ground, decided he did not want to be alone in the woods with whatever had done this to our horses, and followed after the tall, dark, Stranger. I assessed the situation, came to the same conclusion as Catch, and followed after the two men.

"What," I demanded, "what have you neglected to tell us?"

The Snake Stick Man looked over his shoulder at me. "Have you ever heard of the Black Dog of the South Mountain? The Wolf Man of Appalachia?"

I declined to answer.

"Well," said The Snake Stick Man, "now not only have you heard of the Wolf Man of Appalachia, the beast has killed your borrowed gelding, my white mare, and Catch's good jack mule. And at this point, I believe it intends to kill us as well."

The three of us walked forward in silence, The Snake Stick Man taking the lead. Catch and I fell back a few paces and marched shoulder to shoulder, eyes scouring the forest around us.

"No need to worry now," The Snake Stick Man said, sensing our anxiety, "the Black Dog only appears in the night. We are in no danger until the sun sets."

Catch looked my way. "I don't know what worries me more," he whispered, "whatever it was that stalked us through the storm and killed our horses or—"

"Or what?" I asked him, already knowing the answer.

"Or him," Catch breathed as he took a drag off his cigarette and nodded toward the Marshal, The Snake Stick Man, who was making his way through this primeval wilderness with disturbing confidence.

I, too, felt afraid, but, for some reason that I still cannot explain, was totally unable to suggest the most obvious course of action: that we part ways with the Marshal and head home. For every time the thought crossed my mind, the carved wooden eyes of the serpent atop The Snake Stick Man's staff caught mine, and I dismissed retreat completely.

PART II
THE BOOKSTORE FLOODS. WARNE DREAMS. SHOOTOUT AT BARRADALE'S CAMP.

Water soaking through the bottom of my right shoe brought me back from the world of Kephart's book. As I reengaged with my surroundings, the Bookseller spoke.

"Creek's come out of its banks," he said, "flooding the town."

I looked down. Rainwater surged across the road, overwhelming the gutter and seeping under the bookshop door. My shoes were damp from the inch of water that now covered a good bit of the shop floor.

The Bookseller was shoving towels under the doorjamb, but they only stemmed the tide a little. Suddenly, I realized what the low shop ceiling and flood water could mean, and my breath caught in my throat. "We need to get out of here," I said, my voice more panicked than I cared to admit.

"Not out," the Bookseller murmured, "We cannot go out."

He nodded at the deluge of floodwater outside the shop window. It was getting deeper by the second. There was no way we would survive if we went out into the street.

The street lamps were flickering, and parked vehicles were beginning to float, smashing into each other in the floodwaters like some sort of deranged carnival ride.

And then—

That unearthly howl reverberated through the town.

That sound. The howl. I wasn't even sure if it was real or if I was hearing things, but no matter. It stood my hair on end.

And then, I swear. When the lightning flashed. I saw it.

For just a moment, there it was, standing in the middle of the flooded road. Its black hair rippling and standing on end. Its lips curled back and up in a snarl, revealing red, stained teeth. Water foamed and crashed around it's sinewy legs, but it never moved. It just stood there, somehow stronger than the flood, and stared through the window right at me.

And then, in an instant, that thing, it was gone, replaced by a black Honda Civic that careened past, bashed about by the floodwaters. That car was obviously what I had seen, not some supernatural monster. The panic was getting to me, and my eyes were playing tricks. That was all.

I pulled out my cell phone, thinking to call the fire department to see if they could come and get us before things really got out of hand, but I had no service.

"No signal down here," the Bookseller said.

"No signal today?" I asked.

"No signal ever," he answered.

"There had better be another way out of here," I said to the Bookseller. "There's no way I'm gonna drown here in some old bookstore with some guy who, no offense, I don't even know. That is not how I'm gonna go out."

The Bookseller nodded and pointed at the ceiling. "Fair enough. Not my first flood. If it gets real bad, we'll go up."

The Bookseller walked across the shop and opened a door at the back. "This goes to the first floor," he said. "From there, you can get to the second. And if this storm turns biblical, there's a way to the roof from there."

I looked around at the water seeping in and the shelves full of antique literature. "What about your books?" I asked. He shook his head and smiled that strange eternal smile of his.

"Everything has an end," he said quietly.

Outside, it looked like the rain was slowing a bit, and the water wasn't coming under the door as fast. The Bookseller looked out the window, face turned up toward the storm clouds.

I wondered aloud if the storm was calming down any. The Bookseller nodded slightly. "Looks like it's slowin' down a bit."

He took a push broom from behind the counter, wrapped the brush end with a towel, and started nudging water toward a drain in the corner. Watching the Bookseller do physical labor reminded me of how elderly the man appeared to be. "Need some help?" I asked, more than a little concerned for his health.

He smiled. "Don't generally put my customers to work. Go ahead, keep reading. You do your job, and I'll do mine. That's only fair."

Still feeling unnerved but also compelled to keep going with the book, I sat down on the couch and opened Kephart's manuscript back to where I left off.

I looked over my shoulder at the Bookseller, who was still working his push broom, fighting against the trickle of floodwater. If he noticed I was watching him, he didn't show it. Just ignored me and just kept working.

I looked back down at the book.

Nothing better to do while I wait out the flood, I tried to convince myself. But I knew that wasn't all there was to it. Something was driving me, compelling me to keep reading. And that feeling of compulsion was just as frightening as the eerie howls I kept hearing and the strange things I kept seeing.

I took a breath and turned the page.

CHAPTER 3
WARNE'S DREAM

The Snake Stick Man made his way ahead of us, sturdy in his gait despite his use of the sinister walking stick. Catch and I stomped through the brush behind him and tried to make sense of what he had just said. "The hell is he talking about, Kephart?" Catch asked me, his tone hushed.

"You mean the Black Dog of South Mountain?" I offered.

Catch rolled his eyes and rolled another cigarette. "What the hell else would I be talking about, Horace? I mean, I know something killed our horses, but a Wolf Man? Is this Marshal insane?"

I thought for a moment about what Catch had just asked me. You see, I had done quite a bit of reading in the past few years as I traveled the Appalachians. Long days and nights alone, especially in the winter when there is no game about, and the snow is too high to hunt, give a man like me plenty of time to peruse whatever literature I could get my hands on. And peruse I did.

One fine day, my eyes fell across a book written by a certain Madeleine Vinton Dahlgren in 1882 called *South Mountain Magic*. It was an account of the hauntings, monsters, and lost spirits that roamed the Appalachian wilderness. As I have told you, I have always aspired to be a man of faith, and faith in a benevolent God demands faith, or at least belief in its opposite. So I read Madam Dahlgren's account of the sinister and supernatural with what I hoped was an open mind and what I know was an open heart.

But try as I might, I found it difficult to accept anything she had written as possible, let alone plausible. Even her account of the Black Dog of South Mountain, the Appalachian Wolf Man, which was the particular evil our Marshal, The Snake Stick Man had just referenced, seemed utterly ridiculous. And so I would have, at any other point in time than now, have answered Catch in the affirmative. Yes, I would have said, the man must be insane.

But not now.

Not since I saw his staff turn into a living serpent. Not since I saw him bring a dead mountain rattler back to life. And besides, there was that pull in my gut, the grip on my heart that I felt whenever

The Snake Stick Man looked at me. An unexplained draw, attraction, almost like hunger, overrode any intellectual objections I may have had.

"Catch," I said, my tone hushed as well, "we saw him work a miracle yesterday. And I feel something when he is nearby. A draw I cannot escape."

We were headed up a steep incline, fighting our way through dense brush, and Catch saved his breath as he worked his way up the hillside, only remarking this to me.

"I feel it too, Kephart. But that does not mean he is sane."

At last, we three crested the hill and looked out at the valley below us. It was a weird and forbidding land, that valley. Vast labyrinths of rhododendrons covered those profound and dismal depths, impenetrable, sunless in winter, dead but for the murky evergreen of shrubs and spruces. The place was unearthly in its dreariness and desolation. The Snake Stick Man turned to my companion mountaineer and asked if it had a name.

"No, not as a whole," Catch answered.

"Then let us call it Godforsaken," said The Snake Stick Man, "I think God does not often trod upon this land."

Catch nodded in agreement. "A good name," he mused, "it is fitten'."

The Snake Stick Man pointed at a small curl of smoke rising from the valley floor below. "That's where we're headed," he said. "If my sources are correct, the man they call the Sheriff of this area lives down there in yonder cabin."

"Warne?" I choked, "Old Man Warne, is the sheriff here?"

The Snake Stick Man nodded, that strange smile just beginning to cross his lips. "But Ol' Warne is one of the biggest moonshiners this side of hell," I gasped. "How could he be sheriff?"

The Snake Stick Man could contain his smile no longer, and he almost laughed as he grinned at me. "This is a democracy, Kephart. And I suppose the people voted for him."

"What do we need Sheriff Warne for?" Catch growled. "Don't you have warrants for the men we're after?" The Snake Stick Man nodded, reached inside his black coat, and produced three Federal Warrants.

"These are good and legal, but most of the men in this area cannot read, as you well know. But they are good with a rifle and even better to creep up on you in the dark, a skinnin' knife in their hand. And while they cannot read the words a clerk wrote in some federal court miles away from any place they will ever be in all their living days, they may be able to recognize the signature of their good friend and local lawman,

Billy Warne. And that signature may be all that stands between us and a shallow grave out here amongst the mountain laurel."

Suddenly, I realized what The Snake Stick Man was up to, and I shook my head, unable to believe I hadn't realized before. "And Ol' Warne is as crooked as they come, so he'll be sure to know where we can find Buck Ruff and his fellow fugitives."

"Exactly," said The Snake Stick Man, and we continued our descent into the Valley toward Old Man Warne's cabin. But Catch remained unconvinced of our plan. "What if Warne don't wanna talk?" he asked.

"You let me worry about that," was the only answer The Snake Stick Man would give.

I will spare you the details of our approach to Sheriff Warne's cabin other than to say we passed not one, not two, but three moonshine stills on the way toward this so-called lawman's abode. We tripped several alarms as we walked past the moonshine stills toward the cabin, the first being bells hung on tree limbs, the second being string run across a deer path that caused cans suspended in the brush to clank together, and the third being a huge bloodhound of rank and evil temper that hallooed at us from Warne's front porch as Warne himself crept up behind us, muzzle loading rifle to his shoulder and two ancient cap and ball revolvers jammed into his waistband.

When Old Man Warne realized we were not rival moonshiners come to dynamite his operation but rather a group of fellow lawmen, he very near shat himself with surprise and not a little fear. I will tell you this that I have learned from my years in the Appalachians, living among its people. When strangers come to a mountain home and have told who and what they are, then, if the owner likes their appearance even a little bit, he will politely invite them in to rest. Always.

Sheriff Warne did not invite us in.

Instead, he quickly agreed to sign anything The Snake Stick Man put before him. Catch remarked that the man was so rattled at the sight of a true, honest to God US Marshal that he would have immediately signed a warrant for the arrest of his own mother just to get us the hell out of his valley.

Even so, Warne had to allow The Snake Stick Man into his home because that was the only place for miles around that contained something actually resembling a table, and The Snake Stick Man needed a place to write out the new warrants for Warne to sign.

As Catch and I waited outside for The Snake Stick Man to finish writing out warrants, Old Sheriff Warne stood there, leaning against his woodshed, staring at Catch.

His gaze was constant, and his features

unchanging except for the occasional pucker of lips when he spat tobacco juice. Catch leaned toward me and spoke into my ear. "What is his problem?" my friend mused.

"You think Sheriff Warne has a problem?" I responded.

"If not," Catch grunted, "he's about to."

It was at this point that Catch stepped toward the grimacing, greasy-haired, poorly clothed Sheriff Warne and squared off.

"Lookin' at somethin' Warne?" Catch growled.

Warne did not respond. He just kept staring at Catch and occasionally spitting tobacco juice. As you can imagine, this irritated Catch, and he balled his fists up at his side and squared his shoulders. "Don't like havin' an Indian around, do ya Warne? Can't stand a Cherokee on your patch?"

Just as I was sure the two men were about to come to blows, Warne began to shake. His legs gave out from under him, and he sank to the ground, almost lifeless. Catch shot a look over his shoulder back at me, panic in his eyes, suddenly aware of the possible consequences should he be blamed for a white Sheriff's injury.

"I didn't touch him, Kephart. You saw. Didn't lay a finger on the son of a gun," he said.

"I know, Catch. I know."

We approached the immobile Warne and crouched down beside him. Sweat poured off his face and dampened his dirty undershirt. Catch grabbed a nearby jug of 'shine and tipped it up to Warne's lips. "Here, this will bring you round, Warne," he mumbled. "Didn't mean to scare you quite this bad."

Warne managed a few gulps and slowly seemed to come back to his senses. "Forgive me, Catch," he whispered, "I only stared because of the dream."

"What dream?" Catch asked.

Warne took a few more gulps of mountain dew and looked at me and Catch, his eyes bloodshot, darting back and forth.

"You are afoot?" Warne managed at last.

Catch nodded. "Horses dead, yeah?" Warne asked. Catch nodded once more, and Warne covered his eyes with a shaking palm.

"Somethin' come in the night and kilt mine as well. Took their guts from their bellies and dragged it from here to yon. I heard it when it came to my place, a great howl like I ain't never heard in all my days."

"We heard a howl too," Catch offered, "must be a wolf or two still living in these hills."

Just then, Sheriff Warne grabbed Catch by the collar, a desperate fear dancing in his eyes. "No," he breathed, "Weren't no wolf, nor stray hound neither. I saw it. Saw it with my own eyes and then in my dreams, son."

"Saw what? Let go of me," Catch growled, "you're not making any sense." Catch lifted the bottle of 'shine up and nodded toward the apoplectic Warne. "Too much of this rotgut," he spat.

Warne let go of Catch's collar and leaned back against the wall of the log cabin.

"Maybe," he sighed, "Maybe I do drink too much of that there 'shine, but this is the God's honest truth. Last night I saw a Man with hair all about his body... maybe it was a man with hair. Or more like it were a beast, a wolf that walked on two legs and wore a man's clothes...It roared and howled. You heard it. I know you did. Last night, while you waited out the storm. I know you heard it calling out into the darkness. And then I saw it kill my livestock. All of 'em. Come now, Catch. You're from here, an' your family too. Back a thousand years. You must know about the Black Dog of South Mountain."

Catch shook his head and stood up. "Those old legends don't bother me, Warne. I've seen enough of this world to know the old tales you superstitious hillbillies whisper in the dark are of no truth and little interest to me."

But, dear friends, those old tales were of the utmost interest to me. So I offered Sheriff Warne another drink and asked him, "The dream, Warne.

What happened in the dream?"

Warne leaned forward and spoke quietly to me and Catch. "After I saw my livestock laid low by whatever evil that wolf man be, the beast turned toward me and walked to my door, its hair quivering like a rabid dog, overalls soaked in bile and offal, his blood red teeth bared in a hell-bound snarl. I cried out into the darkness for God to save me, but he ain't answered my call. He ain't come and done shit. Instead, the beast lifted me by my collar and threw me against yon doorjamb. Knocked me clean out. And as I lay there on the ground, I dreamed. I dreamed the Wolf Man was about to take me to pieces like he done to my stock when...when..."

At this point, Sheriff Warne lost the thread for a moment and went to sucking on that moonshine jug like it was full of water, and he was dying of thirst. When he finally came up for air, he pointed at Catch with a quivering finger and spoke again.

"Your Marshal. Yon Snake Stick Man appeared and spoke to the beast in a strange tongue. I think he was asking it to come along with him? But the beast roared again and ran off into the brush."

"So you had a dream about the Marshal. So what?" Catch mused.

I had to agree. It seemed quite plausible that our friend Warne had simply drank too much, fallen asleep, and had a strange dream as the storm scared his livestock off.

"No," Warne shook his head, "Never seen that Snake Stick Man in my life. How could I know his face if I never seen him before? He come to me in my dream."

Catch shrugged, still unconvinced. Then the wind shifted, and the stench of death wafted from deep in the woods. Catch and I caught wind of it at the same time and exchanged looks. Warne smelled it, too.

"Go look in the trees, boys. You'll see what's happened to my stock."

As Catch and I turned to go, Warne spoke again. "There's something else, Catch," he whispered, "Something else The Snake Stick Man told me in my dream."

"What?" Catch grunted.

"Your daughter, Catch. The little one your wife lost in childbirth. In my dream, The Snake Stick Man told me he could do for her what he done for the mountain rattler."

Catch lunged at Warne, murder in his eyes. I had to hold him back with all the strength I possessed so great Catch's his rage at these words, but I understood his anger. And his confusion. There were only three of us that knew of his wife's stillbirth. Her, Catch, and I were the only ones who were there when it happened, and we never spoke of it to anyone. I kept silent out of respect for Catch and his wife's feelings, and they kept silent out of grief.

"Liar. Liar," was all Catch could manage to say as I dragged him away from Warne.

"Am I?" Warne replied, "Look in yonder wood and see if I lie about my horse and cow!"

***

Catch and I tried in vain to hold our breath as we stared at the dead animals strewn about the trees. It had taken us a few minutes to walk from Warne'a cabin in the clearing to the edge of the tree line from whence the stench of death emanated, and we were winded. Our exertion made the putrid miasma all the more disturbing and harder to avoid. Neither of us was sure what to believe, but one thing was true: Warne's livestock had been slaughtered in the same vicious manner as ours had been.

Catch and I argued there by the dead animals. I was becoming more and more convinced that this Wolf Man was real and that our Snake Stick Man was no ordinary Marshal. On that point, we agreed, but not for the same reason. Catch was still steadfast in his complete denial of any sort of supernatural explanation for the dead animals, the strange night howling, and for Warne's dream. But he did think The Snake Stick Man was some sort of trickster or confidence man.

Or perhaps a Gypsy conjurer out to frighten simple hillbillies into giving him money.

I was telling Catch that The Snake Stick Man could not be a grifter since he had so far asked no one for any money and that it was Catch and me, not the Marshal, who stood to gain the most financially from this adventure when we heard it.

A single, loud, *gunshot*!

We raced back to Warne's cabin and found poor old Sheriff Warne lying dead on the ground, The Snake Stick Man standing over him, a smoking Luger pistol in his hand.

"What happened?" Catch yelled.

The Snake Stick Man shook his head.

"Our friend here, the crooked Sheriff Warne, was even more corrupt than we had feared, it seems."

The Snake Stick Man pointed at the deceased Warne's hand. A cap and ball revolver was clutched in his lifeless palm.

"The man signed the warrants as I requested, but when I asked him if he knew anything of the whereabouts of the man we search for, he grew sullen and quiet. Then, once my short and friendly, I may add, interrogation ceased, and I turned my back, I heard the rustle of gun metal clearing leather. I turned around to find Warne drawing down on me."

"Then what?" I demanded.

"I shot him, Kephart."

As we stared at the body of old Sheriff Warne, The Snake Stick Man reloaded the empty chamber in his Luger pistol and shook his head. "Do not despair so, my companions. We will still have a story for your publisher, Kephart and your five hundred dollars in bail money, Catch. Before he died, the corrupt Sheriff Warne did say one thing that may help us in our search for the elusive Buck Ruff. Word is the man has been hiding out up at Barradale's Camp. Been cutting lumber with that crew and laying low. So it's off to Barradale's Logging Camp for us three."

And with that, The Snake Stick Man hoisted his saddlebags over his shoulder, took ahold of his serpentine walking staff, and began hiking west. I moved to follow, too rattled to do anything else, but Catch hesitated.

"What if we don't go with you, Marshal?" Catch asked, a steely undertone to his voice.

The Snake Stick Man smiled that terrible smile of his and looked at us. "Then I'd have to shoot you as well for dereliction of duty," he said, "But I don't think I'll have to do that, will I? I know about you, Catch. A deserter you are not."

Catch met The Snake Stick Man's gaze with a strength I know I do not possess. Finally, The Snake Stick Man let his eyes drop. He stared at the ground and looked almost sheepish.

"Warne told you about his dream, did he?"

Catch nodded.

"Me too," The Snake Stick Man breathed, "I did not know about your daughter. And I am sorry that poor excuse for a lawman said such a horrible thing to you. Dredged up those terrible memories. Especially when you are tired and cold and hungry from this, our difficult sojourn into these foreboding hills."

Catch and I looked at The Snake Stick Man as he stood there on the mountainside, rod in hand, black duster coat moving with the cold winter wind, a shadow over his face cast by the brim of his black felt hat. It was odd, for such an imposing man, he looked almost small in that moment.

"Listen, boys," he said, a kind of resignation in his voice, "I cannot do this alone. Buck is a dangerous man, and if my sources are to be believed, these hills are swarming with dangerous men just like him."

It was true. The Sugarlands were notorious for the kind of ruffian that lived there. It was considered by some to be less a geographical area and more an outlaw hideaway.

The Snake Stick Man was correct. We were in danger out here.

"I need your help, Catch," said The Snake Stick Man, "And your's Kephart. This man we seek is a criminal, and I plan to bring him to justice. Will you walk with me?"

Catch said nothing, only picked up his saddlebags and started heading West into the low winter sun. I followed after him, and The Snake Stick Man smiled. It was a smile of relief.

"Good," he said, "And thank you. I'd hate to be alone in these hills. I am truly grateful for your help. Once we arrive at Barradale's Camp, we may relax. I have heard of the place and am told we may expect a friendly reception. Barradale himself is a former US Marshal and will likely help us in any way he can."

We three walked together through the wilderness for quite a while, climbing the mountainside together without any more discussion. After what must have been at least two hours of silence, Catch cleared his throat.

"Didn't take you for the type to scare," Catch said, half to himself and half out loud.

The Snake Stick Man did not immediately respond.

We walked a moment longer before The Snake Stick Man let out a long breath and spoke.

"Well," he said, "I don't generally scare. But I do generally plan on a fair fight. And what we're up against takes three to make fair. Four would be better, but you two are all I have now that Warne is dead."

"Four men to hunt Buck Ruff? You think each of us a quarter tough as one man?" Catch asked, a bit bemused. The Snake Stick Man's expression turned dark, and he spoke quietly as he answered.

"There are forces at work here, truths that I have kept from you men," he said, his eyes scanning the mountainside, piercing the dark shadow of the woods, "and I think now may be the time to tell you. I have held off for fear of driving you away and for the fear that you may think me unhinged. But it was a mistake to withhold what I tell you now."

The Snake Stick Man paused and ran his fingers over the head of his walking stick.

"It gives me no pleasure to say this, but say it I must. You have seen and heard strange things since you began your travels with me," he breathed, "and I believe you will see and hear even more. This, what I am about to say to you, is the latest but not the last. And if you think me a liar who is unacquainted with any true supernatural action, I ask you to remember what I did for the mountain rattler before your very eyes."

The Snake Stick Man took another deep breath before continuing.

"Buck Ruff and this howling monster that the recently deceased Sheriff Warne calls the Wolf Man of Appalachia. It may be the case that they are one and the same. And while you think we are hunting him, hunting it, truly I tell you this: I think Buck has begun to hunt us."

The sounds of Barradale's Logging Camp were just becoming audible through the trees as Catch and I exchanged looks of true concern. But we had no time to express what was on our troubled minds because right as I opened my mouth to speak, we crested a small rise and were met with the sights and sounds of at least a dozen lumberjacks screaming at us.

"Timmmmberrrrr!" they yelled.

I looked up and saw a giant oak falling right on top of us.

CHAPTER 4
SHOOTOUT AT BARRADALE'S CAMP

We had been fortunate. Catch's experience in war had sharpened his reflexes to a razor's edge, and he had grabbed both me and The Snake Stick Man and hurled all three of us just out of harm's way.

The tree had crashed onto the ground with startling force that shook the earth beneath me. As soon as the crunching and snapping of leaves and branches ceased, we could hear the dinner bell ringing up by the tent city these lumberjacks were living in.

Without the slightest concern about our welfare or even a cursory glance in our direction to see if we were still alive, the mob of them quit the work they were about, dropped their axes and mauls, and headed straight for the supper table.

One of them did turn and holler over his shoulder, "Come you three up for chow, if'n you care to eat!" This was the famous Appalachian Mountain hospitality I had expected but not received from Warne. Apparently, mountain people were more concerned with a stranger's stomach than they were with his body or life as a whole.

The Snake Stick Man stood up, brushed himself off, and headed for the camp without saying anything except, "Let's find the one who commands these men. Perhaps he knows which of them is Buck Ruff."

I rolled myself over and sat up. "How do you like that, Catch?" I mused. "Not even so much as a thank you for saving his life. He is, I believe, what they call a cool customer." But I got no answer from Catch. My breath caught in my throat, and I turned to look.

"Catch? Catch."

Much to my relief, I saw my friend standing up alive and not laying down dead as I had feared from his silence. Yet, he looked strange. His hands were shaking, and he seemed unable to catch his breath. He was staring at the scars on his palms that he earned across the sea in the trenches of No Man's Land and mumbling under his breath.

I went to him and touched his shoulder. He pulled away from me as if my palm were a red hot iron.

"Don't," he gasped.

I stood with him while he fought to calm himself. It took a great while, but eventually, his breath returned to normal, and his hands stopped their quivering.

I did not understand at the time but came to learn later on that my dear friend suffered from an ailment common to men who returned alive from that great cataclysm of violence across the sea. Sometimes, when there is a loud sound or a moment of intense danger, their mind will transport them back to the trenches, and it is as if they never left. The mortal danger of the falling tree, the loud yells of the lumbermen, and Catch's quick action that saved my life must have given his nervous system quite a shock.

He spoke through clenched teeth as he rolled himself a cigarette. "My wife — " he gasped, "my son..."

"They are safe," I assured him, "and you are too."

Catch took a long drag off his smoke, shook his head, and looked at his disfigured hands again.

"Never," he whispered, "never."

I stood there watching Catch smoke. He inhaled each time with a quiet, desperate hope but seemed always to exhale in a cloud of despair. I thought of what must be lurking in his mind at all hours, waiting to strike out from the past and take the peace of his present away from him.

"Come," I said, "we are with friends now. A good meal amongst good men awaits us. No danger here. We can relax. These lumbermen will be our allies.

They are employed by a former Marshal. There is but one amongst them who may mean us harm, and he is the man we seek. When they learn this fact, he will for sure be given up to us."

Once Catch recovered, he stomped out the butt of his cigarette, and we walked toward the chow line to see what news our strange Marshal had uncovered about Buck's whereabouts.

"Do not fret, my friend," I said to Catch as we walked, "I believe that oak tree was the last shock of the day."

Catch tried to smile. "I hope so," he said. "Wouldn't that be somethin'? I survive German bombs, bullets, and bayonets only to come home and have some hillbilly drop a tree on me. My wife would be too embarrassed to show her face at the funeral."

We shared a laugh together. "With the help of Barradale and his men, we'll have this Buck Ruff caught before nightfall," I said, "and you'll be home with your family by the end of the week."

I believed it when I said it. But I could not have been more wrong.

As we approached the chow line at Barradale's Camp, we noticed that all the noise had stopped. No clanking of plates, smacking of lips, nor dull roar of conversation. We turned the corner, walked past a few tents, piles of log chains and ax heads, and saw the whole lot of lumbermen, thirty-five or more, sitting or standing in silence and staring at The Snake Stick Man.

I had not noticed before, having only seen them from afar, but these woodsmen were, to a man, a rough and ready bunch. Hard features, scarred faces, armed to the teeth. And they looked enraged. I was at a loss as to what had caused their apparent displeasure.

Catch took a look around at the dirty bunch of angry lumberjacks and cocked his head to the side.

"Good lord, Snake Stick. What'd you say to these boys?"

There was no time to enjoy Catch's joke because before we had a moment to breathe, The Snake Stick Man pulled out his badge and warrants, and as he did so, every lumberjack in that camp pulled a gun.

"They are outlaws," The Snake Stick Man breathed in response to Catch's question.

"All of them?" I croaked as I surveyed the mob of angry woodsmen.

"Yes," The Snake Stick Man affirmed. "Every single one. Apparently."

"I thought you believed the man who owned this camp was sympathetic to our cause?" I said.

"I did," The Snake Stick Man replied, "but I do not anymore."

I noticed Catch was squinting and pointing at each lumberjack, one at a time, and counting.

"Well," he said, "there's about thirty of them. Three for each of us. Ain't that right, Horace?"

"No," I groaned, "You did your math backwards."

"Whaddya mean, backwards?" Catch said.

"It's ten against one," I hissed.

"Aw, hell," Catch said as he cocked his rifle, "I know that. Just tryin' to make you feel better. Plannin' on killin' more than my share anyway. Maybe if you're lucky, Kephart, I'll leave you a few."

"You're funny, Catch," The Snake Sick Man said. "I did not know that about you."

"Yeah, well, I'm full of surprises," Catch grunted. He smiled a sad smile at me and managed a wink as one of the lumberjacks yelled, "Let's shoot the Indian first!"

"Aw, to hell with you, Hillbilly," Catch spat back. "We're gonna shoot the ugly ones first! And your mug is about at the top of that list!"

"Okay, that's enough," The Snake Stick Man growled at us under his breath before yelling to the outlaw lumberjacks, "Drop your weapons in the name of the law!"

But the lumbermen did not obey him. They simply opened fire.

Catch and I dove to the right, aiming for cover behind a pile of logging chains as The Snake Stick Man reached for his Luger pistols, but it was too late.

A load of double-aught buckshot smashed into Catch's torso, tearing flesh and smashing bone. He hit the ground beside me and looked into my eyes as I fired back in a murderous rage, ready to slaughter the animals that had hurt my friend.

"Hang on, Catch!" I hollered, but he said nothing. He just stared at me and bled.

The gunfight raged on with me and The Snake Stick Man giving as good as we got. Mercifully, the lumberjacks had terrible aim, and we managed to retreat. I dragged the incapacitated Catch along the ground with one hand and shot back at our assailants with the other as The Snake Stick Man let go with his two pistols like Zeus throwing bolts of lightning. Every roar of gunfire that erupted from the barrel of his guns hit its mark and sent one of our bearded assailants straight to hell.

We three stumbled down a hill and took cover behind a shaley outcrop, still firing at the enraged men chasing us through the woods.

"What happened?" I demanded. "Why are they shooting at us?"

"Fugitives all!" The Snake Stick Man replied. "I've been lied to. Barradale was no US Marshal. He is a crook. And every son of a bitch in this camp is running from the law! When I mentioned we were a posse, well. You can see the results for yourself."

Catch looked down at his shattered midsection and closed his eyes. "Oh god," he groaned, "I'm dying."

The Snake Stick Man nodded between gunshots.

"Yes, Catch. You are."

We kept firing, The Snake Stick Man and I, but we faced an overwhelming force. The rocky outcropping was protecting us for now. However, the lumbermen were rapidly gaining ground.

"Keep pressure on your wound, Catch!" I screamed between gunshots, but I don't know that Catch could hear me anymore.

"Perhaps we should surrender," I said to The Snake Stick Man.

"Why?" he grunted as he stooped to reload, "so they can kill us easier?"

Suddenly, the gunshots ceased, and the world became quiet save the ringing in my ears.

"What's happened?" I asked.

"They're going to go to the high ground, take positions farther up the mountain. Kill us from above," The Snake Stick Man replied matter of factly.

And it was at that moment when things were the most desperate, we were surrounded by murderous mountain men, backed into a corner, and with my dear friend Catch's lifeblood soaking the dirt, that it appeared.

Hearing that horrid howl and the screams of the Lumberjacks, I peered over the top of the shaley outcrop and saw, with my own eyes, something I fear no one will believe.

There it was. The Black Dog of South Mountain, the Wolf Man of Appalachia. A giant Canid, dressed in torn and stained overalls, standing on its hind legs and tearing the terrified lumberjacks limb from limb.

The Lumbermen turned their guns away from us and trained them on the Wolf Man, but to no avail. If anything, the more they shot, the angrier, stronger... the larger the Black Dog became.

I dropped down behind the rocks and yelled to my companions, "Look!" But there was no answer.

I turned my head to see what kept Catch and The Snake Stick Man from answering me, but I saw nothing. They had disappeared.

I was alone in the Appalachian mountain woods, threatened by a band of violent fugitives and the most terrifying monster you could ever imagine.

And I will tell you, the monster was hungry.

PART III
THE LAW OF THE WILDERNESS

"The backcountry is rough. No boat nor canoe can stem its brawling waters. No bicycle nor automobile can enter it. No coach can endure its roads.

All about me was the forest primeval, where roamed the wild beasts. Bears sometimes raided the fields, and wildcats were a common nuisance. But the beast I had just seen, my god.

I was being hunted. Hunted not only by a band of bloodthirsty fugitives but also by a monster most foul.

And to make matters worse, I was separated from my best friend, my companion, Glenn "Catch" Owl, who himself was somewhere in this godforsaken wilderness, bleeding to death.

His only hope for survival, and perhaps mine as well, was the favor of the mercurial US Marshal, our Snake Stick Man, who I now had come to fear may be more dangerous than all these mountain men and monsters combined.

   I found myself in the Back of the Beyond and could see no way out of it."

CHAPTER 5
THE BACK OF BEYOND

I watched the great beast tear into those rugged mountain outlaws with such furious malice I almost felt sorry for them, even though they had just moments before tried to kill me and my companions.

I looked around me again. I was sure. Catch and The Snake Stick Man had disappeared. As to where, I had no clue.

My attention once again turned to the violent scene unfolding before my eyes. I expected to feel horror but was surprised when a wholly different emotion washed over me...

Many say they find faith through some warm interaction with a congregation or when a feeling of love overwhelms them at the sight of their newborn child. But, to my great surprise, salvation was not offered to me in that manner at all. I did not find it. Rather, it found me in the bloody carcasses of a mountain holocaust.

As I watched the Black Dog of South Mountain, the Wolf Man of Appalachia, work its blood-soaked jaws against the flesh of screaming men, I knew God must exist. What else could be powerful enough to create a monster so terrible?

Enough, I thought to myself. If I am to survive this, I must slip away before either the lumbermen or the monster discover me. I was desperate to find Catch and to somehow save his life. No man loved his family as much as Catch loved his wife and son, and I felt a guilt unimaginable as I slipped over the edge of the shale outcropping I had been hiding behind and dropped to the creek bank below.

The searing pain that coursed up my leg as I landed almost blinded me and stopped my breath in my throat. I covered my mouth and stifled my scream so as not to draw attention to myself. Reluctantly, I looked down and discovered that I, too, had been wounded in the firefight. A load of buckshot had torn my flesh and broken my right leg.

Somehow, I had not realized I was wounded until just now. The adrenaline that coursed through my veins as I had dragged Catch out of camp while firing back at the lumbermen must have masked the pain. That mask had fallen away now and was replaced with an agony I can not adequately convey. I will say this:

if the horror of the Wolf Man had not convinced me there was an opposite to the Almighty, this pain in my broken and bleeding leg may very well have done the trick.

I took my knife from my belt, cut a strip of cloth out of my overcoat, and fashioned a crude tourniquet and splint from a stray stick.

This was a slow and difficult procedure. Pulsing pain washed over me as I grappled with my broken bone and the ripped skin it had penetrated. Waves of nausea threatened to knock me unconscious. The blood on my hands ruined my grip, and the bit of overcoat I had cut slipped through my shaking fingers as I tied knots.

Finally, after several tries, the splint was made and attached.

I could not walk, that was for sure. So I tossed anything I felt I could get by without to lighten my load and started crawling. I kept the six-shooter in my holster, a few cartridges in my pocket, and the knife tucked into my belt. I hoped, but did not believe, these items would be enough to sustain me.

The sounds of murder from Barradale's Camp had faded and were replaced by the eerie quiet of the mountains. The dribble of the half-frozen creek and the shuffling of winter brown leaves that still clung to branches in the cold Appalachian wind did little to mask my grunts as I dragged my body across the mountainside. I was so loud as to make myself a target, and I knew it.

That fact was made all too obvious when I heard the footsteps, those of a wolf's paw slinking through the leaves.

I stopped moving, afraid even to breathe.

And there it was. In the trees in front of me. Crouched on all fours now, not standing like before, it was perhaps more frightening. Perhaps not. It is difficult to quantify fear. In any case, it slinked over to me the way a wolf does as it approaches for the kill.

I felt its hot breath on my skin. The metallic bite of blood and death covered the beast's clothes and hair. I tasted its warmth in my mouth.

So close it was. On me like a murderous lover.

I closed my eyes and waited.

Hot blood-breath wheezed in my ear. I waited for its great maw to close over my neck, but it did not. Instead, the beast spoke.

"*Help*," it said.

"Help you?" I gasped, unable to disguise my shock.

"*Help*," it growled again.

"Very well," I sputtered, "what would you have me do?"

"Let him die. Let him die..." it said.

I was so shocked by the monster's statement I turned around to look at the beast, my terror be damned.

But when I opened my eyes, the Wolf Man was gone.

I lay on the cold ground and wept silently for a good long while before continuing my slow crawl across the mountain.

It was strange, I thought as I shivered in the cold. I felt in a hurry. Night was closing in, and the temperature was dropping, but I did not know where I was crawling to. I only knew that I must go on, even if that meant simply to die in motion. That was better than sitting still to wait.

I did not make good time or good distance, so great was my pain and debilitating my injuries, both physical and mental. The low, deep growling of the Wolf Man echoed in my mind with every miserable inch of frozen ground I drug myself over.

Help...

What did it mean? This agent of death, this unholy beast covered in the blood and entrails of human men, asking me for help? And why had it spared me when it had so recently, only moments before, ended the lives of so many others?

And if the Black Dog wanted something dead, why not just kill it itself?

Soon, the sun fell below the mountain top, and it was dark. Not long after, the temperature became unbearable. My thoughts turned from the pain in my leg from the gunshot wound and the pain in my arms from dragging myself across the shaley mountain ground to the dull ache of cold. I could go no further.

I lay on the ground and thought first of my death, then as I weakened, of Catch and his family. Where was my friend? Had he died already? No. In my heart of hearts, somehow, I knew he was still with us, and I rallied my body for one last try. If Catch was still alive, I must survive and try to find him.

I *would* find him.

So I took three deep breaths, raised my head, and tried to move once more. But my injured leg had become tangled in a berry vine, and when I dragged myself forward, the pain from the sudden jerk backwards on my broken femur knocked me clean out. I lay unconscious on the mountainside, nearer to death than ever I had been.

CHAPTER 6
THE GRANNY WOMAN

I woke with a start and blinked to clear my blurred vision. As the sleep fell from my eyes, I could see I was in a small cabin. Well, more a lean-to or shack than a true cabin. It was dark and cramped, but thank the Lord, it was warm. A fire crackled in a primitive hearth, and a diminutive figure was crouched over a pot that bubbled and boiled.

She, for I could just tell it was a woman under that dirty, ragged calico, was stirring whatever was in the old black pot slowly and mumbling to herself.

I could not make out what she was saying, but the rhythm and meter of the sound suggested, to my ears anyway, a prayer. Or a spell. I tried to lift my head and speak, but she must have heard me because before I opened my mouth, she raised her hand, without looking away from her cook pot, and spoke.

"Don't move ye none," she rasped, "Hit's a

bad break have you in yon leg. And black pison in yer blood."

She spoke with the strongest affectations of Mountain Speech that I had yet come across in my time in the Appalachians. And her gravely voice struck fear into my heart, so harsh was its timbre.

She turned to face me, an earthenware bowl of that bubbling brew in her hand. Her hair was white, and her face was a sunbaked brown even this late in the year, a testament to the time an isolated mountain woman spends outdoors in her quest to survive.

She stood up and moved toward me.

Her spine was crooked from years of backbreaking labor, and her gait uneven, but her eyes shone bright blue. They were the only part of her that seemed younger than the mountain on which she made her home.

I had been told stories about women like this, the one in whose home I now was a guest. There is a term for these aged mountain women who live even more isolated lives than the rest of their Appalachian kin. Wise and experienced, these "Granny Women," as they are called, know all the secrets a mountaineer needs to survive. They can cure sick livestock, assist a woman in a difficult birth, and concoct all manner of healing potions.

They also generally have a deep knowledge of

the black arts, so it is wise to keep them a friend and never make one an enemy.

And so this Granny Woman kneeled before me and wordlessly offered a drink of that potion she had been stirring when I first awoke. I could not help myself. I hesitated. My stalling was met with a stern glare.

"Drink, you," she commanded. So I did.

You may wonder what the drink tasted of, but in truth, I cannot tell you. I have no memory of the taste, only that it was warm.

"How did I come to be in your home, ma'am?" I asked after swallowing her brew.

She said nothing, only stood up, limped back to her chair by the fire, and sat. I noticed now that there was some type of small animal roasting on a spit above the flames. The Granny Woman began turning the spit, roasting whatever it was with the kind of patience only the elderly possess.

"What have you given me to drink?" I continued. She said nothing, kept turning her spit, and pointed commandingly at the bowl I held in my hands. I nodded and took another sip of the draught.

"For yon leg, it is," she said. "Have you up and about by daybreak."

I looked down at my injured appendage. The Granny Woman had wrapped it in a poultice and must have set the bone while I was yet unconscious. I was impressed with her skill but did not believe I would be on my feet anytime soon.

"Aught call you Thomas the way you doubt," she said, turning the spit and seeming to read my thoughts, "but what is your given name, son?"

"Horace," I told her, "and while I do doubt I will walk in the morning, I sincerely hope to be incorrect. Now, tell me. How did I come to be here in your home?"

Again, the Granny Woman seemed to ignore my question. She cut off a piece of the roasted animal and brought it to me on a tin plate. "Ain't much," she croaked, "but I'll share with ye what I do have."

It was not until she set the food before me that I realized how hungry I had become. I tucked into the meal and was surprised at how good it tasted. I felt better with food in my stomach, and the ache in my leg was less severe than before. As I ate, I managed to ask the Granny Woman about Catch. I told her about the shootout at Barradale's Camp, Catch's injury, and that I was looking for him and The Snake Stick Man. I did not mention the Black Dog of South Mountain. I felt that broaching the subject of the Wolf Man may have been too much even for this mountain mystic. So I left it out. But had she seen Catch? Heard or seen anything that might help me find my friend before it was too late?

The Granny Woman's gaze dropped to the dirt floor, and she shook her head.

"Truly. You do not recall, do you," she asked, "how you come to be here, in my home?"

I shook my head, no.

"I've a few things to tell you, Horace. I do not know yet that you are ready to hear them." Her voice, so strong before, was little more than a whisper now.

Fearing the worst about Catch, I implored the Granny Woman to tell me what had become of my friend. At last, she acquiesced. She turned to me and placed her hands in her lap, clasping her fingers together and nodding her head.

"It were the Black Dog what brought you here to me, Horace."

"What?" I exclaimed. "The Wolf Man of Appalachia? Brought me here."

"Yes, cradled in his arms," she said, her face solemn and drawn, "and after he dropped you here, he took me to a cave acrost yon holler and made me to listen to what was happenin' inside. Two men in there 'hit was, and what I heard between them, I must tell you now. That is, if'n you are ready to hear it."

I told her that I was ready and desperate for any news of my friend. "Very well," she sighed, "I wish't it were different, but the news I have for you...it ain't good."

And now, dear reader, I will relate to you what the old Granny Woman told me she saw and heard while she eavesdropped at the mouth of the cave across the holler.

CHAPTER 7
DEVIL'S BARGAIN

The cave was made of limestone. A great dark hole carved into the side of the ancient mountain by the persistent, unyielding action of billions of drops of water over millions of years. Even now, water yet trickled down the side of the limestone, taking tiny bits of the mountain with each drop.

She saw him, our friend Catch, inside that mountain's maw, lying against the old cave's wall. Blood from his wound was pooling below him and mixing with the drops of water, staining the bedrock floor. The Snake Stick Man stood next to him, keeping vigil, leaning against that sinister, serpentine walking stick of his.

He carried a lantern to light the dark, and it cast black, dancing shadows. But, the Granny Woman told me, The Snake Stick Man's shadow did not appear in the same shape as he did.

As the lantern's flame flickered, the dark outline behind him was not of a duster coat and cowboy hat. Instead, a sinewy body crowned with a set of black horns danced across the cave wall behind our Snake Stick Man. And the serpent at the head of his walking stick, while in reality made of carved wood, had a shadow that curled and hissed as a live snake would, even as the wooden rod remained stone still in his hand.

"Wake, Catch," she heard The Snake Stick Man command, "we have something to discuss."

Catch opened his eyes, somehow roused from the torpor of imminent death, and looked around at the cave first with confusion, then anger.

He managed a question.

"Why are we in this cave?"

The Snake Stick Man stood up and pointed at the cave wall with his walking stick, the shadow of the snake's tongue tasting the dank subterranean air.

"To be closer to where I come from."

At this moment, the Granny Woman said Catch tried to stand but lost his footing in the muck of his own blood and fell backwards, landing in a painful slump upon the ancient stone, unable to escape. The Snake Stick Man casually ignored this attempt to flee and spoke once more.

"These mountains are old, Catch," The Snake

Stick Man continued, "the first to reach their peaks up toward the sky. But they are the most worn down, and their caverns and caves reach deep into the earth. And once this water, this cool water that takes the stone and turns it to emptiness one tiny drop at a time, once it digs deep enough—"

At this point, the Granny Woman said The Snake Stick Man paused his speech, knelt down next to Catch, and pressed his hand deep into Catch's wound.

"—once deep enough, I can dig myself out. And become free."

The sound poor Catch made, the wail of unspeakable agony as The Snake Stick Man's fingers wrapped around his innards, was more than the Granny Woman could bear to describe. Instead, she told me this: I never wish to hear such again, as many or as few days as I still have left on this earth.

The Granny Woman told me this as well: when The Snake Stick Man knelt down to hurt poor Catch, his shadow did not. Instead, the shadow of a horned beast with a real serpent in its hand stayed upright on the cave wall.

And it danced.

After what seemed an eternity of pain, The Snake Stick Man released his grip on Catch's intestines and stood. His shadow remained detached from him and started to creep slowly toward the mouth of the cave. Catch did his damndest to catch his breath and subsequently asked The Snake Stick Man a question that had been on both our minds for some time.

Catch squinted at the strange man dressed all in black.

"What are you?"

The Snake Stick Man looked Catch in the eye and smiled.

"White men call me Ol' Scratch. Or Demon. Or Devil. Your people, the Cherokee, might say I am the One Dressed in Stone. They are all equally close to the truth. And equally far from it."

Catch stared back at The Snake Stick Man with a boldness that surprised the eavesdropping Granny Woman and answered The Snake Stick Man thusly, "I do not believe in any of that."

The Snake Stick Man smiled again, the grimace that parted his lips even more forbidding than before and laughed. His horned shadow, now several feet away from him, creeping toward the mouth of the cave, threw its head back in a silent, mocking cackle.

"Oh, my dear Catch," The Snake Stick Man's voice was smooth like oil, "it matters not if you believe. Because, as you can see, whether you be my servant and full of faith or a skeptic full of doubt, it makes no difference. I yet exist."

The Snake Stick Man launched himself down

again and kneeled at Catch's side. He cradled Catch's head in his hands and pulled his face close.

"Do you wish to see your family again?" The Snake Stick Man asked, "Do you?"

It was at this moment that the poor old Granny Woman realized the disembodied Shadow had crept up upon her and was staring at her with missing eyes, hidden behind a darkness too deep to describe. She was so afraid she was unable to move, even to fall to her knees and weep, though her legs shook like leaves in a windstorm.

The Shadow turned its horned head and held a hand to its gaping black maw as if to shout, but no sound could be heard except by The Snake Stick Man, who turned his head and answered the apparition's call.

"Yes," he hissed, "I know she is there. It is as I wish it to be. I need the Granny Woman to see."

Catch, growing weaker by the second, tried with all his might to escape The Snake Stick Man's clutches, but to no avail. Finally, he managed a reply.

"If I die, I die. My family knows I love them. There is no unfinished business between us. Only love for my wife. And love for my son. Nothing has been left undone. Nothing left unsaid."

The Snake Stick Man's face became uncharacteristically red with emotion, and he fairly spat his answer.

"Lies!" he cried. "What about your little girl?"

Catch began to weep at the sudden flood of memories the mention of his stillborn daughter brought back to him. His pain made The Snake Stick Man smile and caused the Shadow to toss its horns back in a silent peal of horrible, inaudible laughter.

"Yes, yes..." The Snake Stick Man growled, "This is why you followed me into the wilderness. This is why you agreed to come."

"No...no," Catch gasped, "the money. I need the bail money, the reward for Buck's capture."

The Snake Stick Man shook his head. "You lie, Catch," he purred, "I know why you came. You saw what I did for the dead mountain rattler. And you think I can do the same for the dead infant girl that lays buried in your wife's garden beneath the gnarled branches of a dogwood tree."

The Snake Stick Man threw down his staff, and as it hit the cave floor, it again transformed into a real, live serpent. It hissed and spat as it coiled itself around the bleeding and immobile Catch. The Horned Shadow began to dance an ancient dance and wail soundlessly on the cave wall, clapping its black hands in silent, satanic delight.

"Do you not understand, Catch?" cooed The Snake Stick Man, "It is within your power to save yourself. You may stand up and walk out of this cave if you wish. You may walk this earth all the rest of your natural days, hand in hand with your wife and son."

"No. You lie," Catch spat.

The Shadow stopped its dance long enough to shake its horned crown "no" and wag a finger with petulant dissatisfaction at Catch's protestations before returning to its bizarre gyrations.

"There is only a small price you must pay for the privilege of my miracles," The Snake Stick Man continued. He turned and sat down next to Catch, cradled Catch's head in his lap, and stroked Catch's face with loving tenderness. "Only a small price. A gift in return, you might say."

The Shadow turned and kneeled beside Catch. It reached out its arms and pulled them back, over and over, in a universal gesture for "give to me, give to me, give to me."

The Snake Stick Man's Staff had crawled halfway up Catch's body now, and its tongue flickered near Catch's face.

"What," Catch gasped, "what is your price? What do you need to let me live and bring my daughter back?"

"Two things you must know," The Snake Stick Man mused, still stroking Catch's face as his Snake Staff hissed and his Shadow danced, "First, while your daughter will live again, you will never know her."

"Never?" Catch asked.

"No, never," The Snake Stick Man answered. "It must be enough to know that she will be born again to a different woman and man than you and your wife. But she will exist, and live, and learn, and love, and breathe the air and swim the water and walk the face of this earth. That I swear to you. But you will never meet her, nor touch her, nor call out to her by her name, as long as you yet live."

Catch looked down at the hissing snake on his chest, then up at The Snake Stick Man, who was still caressing his pallid cheek.

"What is the second part? The other half of your price?"

The Snake Stick Man sighed and looked deep into Catch's eyes. "You will be mine. Willingly and without hesitation. When I ask and how I ask. There are those who have made this promise to me and subsequently changed their minds. You must understand there are consequences for such an action."

Catch lifted his hand and pantomimed smoking a cigarette. The Snake Stick Man nodded, reached into Catch's pocket, and retrieved his tobacco and rolling papers.

"I had believed," The Snake Stick Man said as he opened the tobacco pouch and spilled some of the noxious weed onto the small square of paper he held between his fingers, "that you only smoke when you are afraid. Are you now afraid?"

Catch looked at the serpent on his chest, the devilish Shadow on the cave wall, and then back at The Snake Stick Man.

He nodded.

"Shitless."

"It is only natural, Catch, to be afraid," The Snake Stick Man soothed, "but I must say, you are facing this all with the greatest sense of calm I have yet witnessed. And I must tell you, I have been through many of these."

"Thanks, I guess," Catch grunted.

The Snake Stick Man smiled. He rolled the tobacco up and held the cigarette to the mouth of his dancing Shadow. The Shadow leaned down and blew upon the end, which, to Catch and the Granny Woman's great surprise, caught fire and glowed. The Snake Stick Man offered the now lit cigarette to Catch, who took it between his lips and inhaled deeply.

Just then, Catch began to cough and wheeze. Blood dribbled down from his now colorless lips. The Horned Shadow stopped its dance and pointed to Catch's chest with animated concern.

"Yes, yes, I see," The Snake Stick Man answered, "the blood is in his lungs now. There is not much time.

You hear me, Catch? Soon, you will be beyond my ability to save. What is your decision? Die? Or see your family again and give your daughter new life?"

The Granny Woman told me Catch remained silent but that she could see the pain in his eyes as he felt his life slipping away. He tortured himself, she said, seesawing between his desire to see his family again and his firm belief that this was all a wild hallucination only granted legitimacy by his oxygen deprived brain.

"No," she wished to cry out, "Don't you give the devil your soul!" But she was unable to speak or even to move. Some evil kept her pinned to the ground, trapped at the mouth of the limestone cave, and forced to bear unwilling witness.

Finally, as the life slipped from his eyes and the cigarette from his lips, she heard Catch whisper.

The Granny Woman said Catch spoke words to The Snake Stick Man with his dying breath, but he was so weak, his speech so hushed, that she could not make out, and therefore could not tell me, what it was that he had said.

CHAPTER 8
A DARK SUNRISE

It is only a town-dreamed allegory that represents Nature as a fond mother suckling her young upon her breast. Those who have lived close to wild Nature know her for a tyrant, void of pity and of mercy, from whom nothing can be wrung without toil and the risk of death.

As I lay there on the floor of the Granny Woman's cabin, I was struck at the truth of nature's cruelty. This evil, this Snake Stick Man, is of the earth and, therefore, of nature. And whatever gifts he offers, whatever miracles he provides, they come at a cost disproportional to the greatness of his deed. So, for Catch, the mortal life of his daughter would cost him the immortal soul he does not even believe he possesses.

The Granny Woman was still seated in front of me, stirring the pot in the hearth. She had stopped speaking, and her face was like stone. The cook fire cast her shadow against the log wall of the cabin, and it grew and shrank with the flicker of the flames.

"Is that all?" I cried, "What else can you tell me of my friend? Did he agree? Has he sold his soul?"

She did not answer, only shook her head.

"Oh, God," I moaned, "It is my fault. He never would have left on this godforsaken manhunt if I had not encouraged it."

I sat there, unconsolable, thinking of Catch's poor wife and son and of Catch. Had he sold his soul? It was unspeakable to imagine, and I was lost in dread when a sound in the dark valley below, the howl of the Wolf Man, roused me.

"Wait," I said, my mind suddenly ablaze with questions, "you said the Wolf Man brought me here. And that he brought you to the cave?"

The Granny Woman's hands clasped each other in a state of nervous fidgeting, but her face remained as placid as ever. A small nod was her only answer.

"And this is the same Wolf Man, the same Black Dog of South Mountain, that attacked the outlaws at Barradale's Camp when they began to shoot at us?"

Again, the Granny Woman nodded, then tried to change the subject. "How is your leg, Horace?"

I gave it a wiggle and was surprised to discover that it felt nearly well, but I pushed that thought from my mind and concentrated on the question at hand.

"Much better, thank you, but why did the Wolf Man defend us. And how do you know him?"

Suddenly, what must be the truth occurred to me, but I could not believe it possible. So I continued with a barely contained excitement tempered with fear.

"What is your name, madam?" I asked. She declined to answer. "Please," I said, "you must tell me your name."

The Granny Woman's hands held each other so tightly now that her knuckles had turned white. But still, she would not answer. So I did.

"You are Mee Maw Ruff, aren't you. Buck's grandmother?"

You see, I had heard tell that the old matriarch of the Buck clan did live on her own in a shack in the Sugarlands and that she was an honest and true Granny Woman, the mountain people's name for a white witch.

Again, the Granny Woman nodded.

"Buck is the son of my son, yes," she said, "And he got himself in a spot of trouble with your Snake Stick Man years ago. And he took from him his soul the same way he took 'hit off'n your friend, Catch. And my boy, my Buck, he was cursed to walk this earth when the night is dark as the Black Dog. As the Wolf Man of Appalachia."

"My lord, woman," I gasped, "That is how he escaped from his prison cell. No man with ordinary strength could have done what he did. Tore that iron bed frame apart and knocked a hole in a sturdy brick wall."

"Yes, yes, it be true what you're sayin', Horace," the Granny Woman nodded but looked increasingly uncomfortable. "Tell me, Horace, think you now to be able to stand on that leg?"

I put a little weight on my injured leg and was once more shocked to realize that the potion the Granny Woman had given me seemed to have worked. There was almost no pain now. But again, I pushed that thought from my mind and continued my questioning.

"And that is how Buck escaped detection all those weeks in the hills, with all those Marshals after him. And the dead bloodhounds. That was him?"

"Yes, but Horace, listen to me —"

"Then why was The Snake Stick Man searching for him? Why did we go on this journey? Wait. The Wolf Man, it asked me for help. Does it need my help to escape The Snake Stick Man?"

It was at this point the Granny Woman's patience with me gave way.

"Damn you, you chatty sonumbitch!" she roared, "Listen to me. Horace. You can disobey Ol' Scratch up to a point. Just so much. That's why my

Buck run off from him, and that's why Snake Stick was a' searchin' after him. But you can disobey only to a point. And when The Snake Stick Man was in danger, when them lumbermen was a firin' on you, that's when my Buck could ignore the call no longer and had to help your Snake Stick Man."

It was a lot for me to take in, and I was momentarily rendered uncharacteristically silent. But I noticed a change in the Granny Woman. The old woman's eyes were darting back and forth now, fear visible in them for the first time.

"What?" I asked, "What is wrong?"

"You can trick him. That's how it's done, Horace. That's how you help my Buck and save your friend."

It was getting light outside, but it stayed dark in the windowless cabin, the only illumination inside the structure being a soft glow emanating from the embers of the cook fire. I looked out the doorway and noticed a white circle of ashes surrounding the cabin. The Granny Woman's eyes followed my gaze out the doorway.

"Only until sunrise, then it don't work no more," she rasped.

"What will no longer work?"

"Yonder circle of ashes. What all keeps the devil from here. From me." The Granny Woman looked me straight in the eye. "Tricks, Horace. Remember that.

It's the only way."

I was about to ask her what she meant when I noticed something strange. The sun was creeping above the trees now, but as I said, the cabin was still dark as pitch, and the cook fire cast the Granny Woman's shadow against the far log wall.

Except it was her shadow no longer.

A Horned Beast appeared in her shadow's place and lunged at me.

"Get you away, Horace!" the Granny Woman cried.

I leapt to my feet, grateful for my magically healed leg. Two shadowy hands came at me from the darkness. I dodged them and sprang for the cabin door.

Once outside, I could see the horned Shadow turn its ire on the Granny Woman. Her screams overwhelmed my senses as I watched the Shadow grab her and pull her out of sight.

Then her screaming stopped.

The eerie mountain silence was more disquieting than the Granny Woman's death wail had been. I felt an unease deep in my gut, a primal fear. The sort of animal instinct that warns prey of the presence of its predator.

This is it, I thought. The Law of the Wilderness. Eat or be eaten. Take or be taken. I knew in my bones I was in great danger, so I resolved to flee.

But I did not have time to go anywhere because as I spun around and turned heel to run, there he was, standing right behind me.

"Horace," The Snake Stick Man whispered in the misty gray dawn, "I have been looking for you."

I knew I should feel terror as his hand clasped my shoulder in an iron grip, but I did not.

I felt nothing.

"Come," The Snake Stick Man offered, his serpentine staff of hand-carved wood in one palm, my arm in the other, "you must be hungry. Let us go eat."

As The Snake Stick Man led me deeper into these Appalachian hills, deeper than any man with good sense would ever willingly go, I knew I should have felt fear. But as I said, I did not. Instead, I was empty. And do you know why, dear reader? Because, in that moment, I realized I had no earthly idea what to do. My mind was blank.

I thought back on the stories and legends I had spent so many cold mountain nights reading by candlelight and could think of none that would help me.

I was at a total loss. I did not know what to do.

For perhaps the first time in my life, I did not have a plan. I could see no way forward. So I prayed and hoped I would discover one and have the chance to enact it before my soul, as well as the soul of my dear friend Catch, was forfeit to this evil, this Devil, this Snake Stick Man.

But I must confess, I was in no way confident I would find a way to succeed.

I came to realize, as I walked beside The Snake Stick Man that morning, that I was damned.

PART IV
MOONSHINELAND

I slammed the book shut, unwilling to read further. I couldn't say exactly why, but Kephart's writing was starting to freak me out. And make me angry.

Thunder and rain pounded the bookshop. I looked through the window. Outside, I could see the water rising again. It made me nervous. There's so much power in nature. If nature chooses to take us, I mean really decides our time is up, then, honestly, we are helpless. It was strange, but that was the same exact feeling the book was giving me.

"Storm's picking up steam," the Bookseller whispered, "Hoped the worst was over, but I was wrong."

I realized the Bookseller was standing behind me, reading over my shoulder. I twisted around to look at him, a little upset and, frankly, creeped out that he had been standing so close to me without saying anything. His face was different. Still had that eternal quality, but it was darker somehow.

"You stopped reading," he said.

I nodded, yes. The Bookseller looked pained.

"Why?" he asked.

I couldn't really say.

Sure, the storm and flood were distracting, and this entire situation was strange and getting stranger by the second, but that was not why I had stopped. There was something deep inside of me that recoiled at each word, every new paragraph. Not in horror or disgust. It was more like catching your reflection in the mirror and disliking what you see. It was unnerving. I just didn't want to keep going. But that's not what I said to the Bookseller.

"I don't believe a word of this," I said to him. "No wonder his publisher refused to print it. Magic Granny Women? The Devil in a cave? Wolf Man? It's salacious, made-up junk. A grab bag of old Appalachian superstitions."

The Bookseller just looked at me, a sadness in his eyes.

"You believe so, huh?" He shook his head and scratched his face, waiting for my answer.

I nodded. I did think so. What was written here in this lost edition of *Our Southern Highlanders* was preposterous. I had read the final version of Horace

Kephart's book, and I could see the similarities, but this earlier version was obviously fiction that the man had tried to pass off as a memoir.

There was a bright flash of light, sharp and white. Lightning again.

This last bolt was close. Very close. It flashed bright, almost blinding me, and its thunder rattled the floorboards of the old shop. As my vision returned, I saw the Bookseller was still behind me, his finger raised, jaw set, face expressionless and unmoving, like it was carved out of stone.

He was pointing out the window.

That's when I saw it. For real, this time.

I lost my breath and started shaking. There was no denying it now. I was either witnessing something fantastic, or I had lost my mind.

It stood on two legs and wore ripped denim overalls but was covered in hair and had a snout and pointed ears. Teeth stained blood red. Its eyes were yellow, like amber.

It was what I had thought I'd seen chasing me into the bookshop but refused to acknowledge. It was what I had been catching glimpses of this entire storm but had refused to believe I saw. But there it was, right across the street from me, soaking in the rain.

The Bookseller touched my shoulder and whispered in my ear, "Don't worry."

"Don't worry?" I spat back at him, "Is that supposed to make me feel better?"

He nodded a bit sheepishly.

"Well," I growled, one eye on the Bookseller and the other watching the clothed animal stalking us from across the street, "it's not working."

"It can't cross water," he said, confidence in his voice, "We are safe as long as the weather holds."

"Great," I moaned, "If the rain stops, at least we won't drown, we'll just be eaten by a friggan Wolf Man."

The Bookseller nodded curtly. "That is correct."

"What does it want?" I asked, afraid of the answer to my own question.

"Keep reading."

The Bookseller's voice had lost a bit of its former swagger. Watching that half-man, half-animal pace back and forth across the road was taking its toll on his confidence.

"The answer is in the book," he continued. "Finish it. While there is still time."

I looked down at the book in my lap. Every fiber in my being was screaming at me. Run. Get away. But that same strange feeling of compulsion came back and drove me on.

Try as I might, I could not stop myself. The terror I felt was powerful but not powerful enough to overcome this other feeling. This compulsion to stick around.

Why in God's name did I want to stick around? I racked my brain for an answer.

What the hell is wrong with me? Am I insane? Have I got a death wish?

No. It was none of that. I realized the thing driving me to read and compelling me to hang around this Bookshop was the same thing that made me study journalism in college and stay in a low-paying job at a small local newspaper.

I wanted to know what was really going on. I always want to know what's really going on. And if I left now, I would never know what was pacing and howling as it stalked us from across the floodwater.

I picked up the book, took a deep breath, and opened it back up.

CHAPTER 9
BREAKFAST WITH THE DEVIL

I walked alongside The Snake Stick Man. His face was placid as always. His gait was not fast, nor was it slow. Everything was as it would usually be, which I found most disturbing. Because after what had happened last night, nothing could possibly be the same.

I opened my mouth several times, intending to speak, but refrained in every instance. I could not bring myself to utter anything but a deep, shuddering sigh.

In a short while, we came upon Catch, who had built a small fire and was cooking breakfast. Eggs and fried apples, I think it was.

You cannot imagine my surprise at the state my dear friend Catch was in.

He was well.

No sign of his wound, no blood on his skin. Nothing. All that remained as evidence of his near death were his clothes. They were torn, shredded, in fact, anywhere on his torso where the buckshot had entered his body.

Catch looked up as we approached. Then he smiled at me.

"Mornin', Kephart," he chirped, "where you been all night? We were worried about you."

I was unnerved, to say the least.

Did he not remember? Did he not wish to say anything in front of The Snake Stick Man? Or had he lost his mind.

"My dear Catch," I managed to blurt out, "your —" I pointed at Catch's torn jacket, waistcoat, and shirt, "your wound."

The Snake Stick Man saw me staring at Catch's torso and heard me fighting to speak. He knelt down beside the fire and helped himself to a bit of what Catch was cooking.

"There is no wound, Horace," he purred.

"But," I protested, "I saw him shot. I saw you shot, Catch. I carried you from the field, mortally wounded. Bleeding like a stuck hog."

"And yet," The Snake Stick Man spoke, his mouth full of breakfast, "you see he is not shot."

Now, you must understand, dear reader, although I had just witnessed a strange shadow demon attack me and the Granny Woman, and even though I was now myself walking on a broken leg that had been healed overnight by mountain magic, I still could not quite believe what I was witnessing. This was not a lack of faith or a stubbornness, or even a desire for things to be different.

It was none of that.

As a matter of truth, I wanted the magic to be real. I had been searching these hills for the kind of mystic truths these past few days had uncovered. Years ago, when my life had turned sour after my wife and child had abandoned me, I had at first wished for and then come to believe that there could be more to this world than meets the eye. More to this life than the simple pleasures that work and family bring. And more to this life than the agony and pain those same institutions rain down upon us.

There must be more, I had thought to myself. And so I will go out into these primeval hills and search for it.

So you see, I wanted to believe that Catch's wound was no more. Even if the power that had healed him was the darkest this universe had as yet vomited forth from the ancient void, I still wanted it to be true.

But my eyes, try as they might, could not convince my mind that what they saw was real.

The Snake Stick Man was watching me, chewing his breakfast and holding his walking staff, running his fingers over the head of the wooden serpent

RYAN MICHAEL HINES

that crowned the top of this, his constant traveling companion.

"Very well," he said, apparently reading my mind, "place your hand on him and feel with your fingers what your eyes refuse to acknowledge."

"No, no, I think that is not necessary," I managed to say as I sat down next to Catch and reached for one of the tin plates beside the cookfire.

"Do it now, Kephart."

This was the first time I had ever heard The Snake Stick Man raise his voice, and it sent fingers of ice up my back and into the base of my skull. I looked over at Catch, who was seated beside me.

"Catch," I whispered, terrified.

"Not now," was all he said as he turned to me and offered his body. Reluctantly, I lifted my hand and brought it towards Catch's clothed torso. As I did, I swear to you the tongue of the serpent at the top of The Snake Stick Man's walking staff flickered, tasting my fear on the air.

I looked at Catch, suddenly aware of how uncomfortably close my face was to his.

"It's alright," he said. "Go ahead."

The Snake Stick Man watched me as my fingers descended deeper, finding their way through layers of shredded textile. I expected at any moment to feel the warm wet of blood or the strange slip of intestine.

But all I felt when my hand finished its journey was Catch's skin.

I was flabbergasted and felt around and around, searching for some evidence of the shotgun blast that had nearly taken my friend's life. But I felt nothing except Catch's hand pulling mine away.

"Easy, Kephart," he said, "that shit tickles."

The Snake Stick Man was still staring at me, and his staff was still tasting my terror on the breeze. I sat in dumbstruck silence for a moment. Then I heard The Snake Stick Man whisper, "Oh ye of little faith. Now, do you believe?"

I looked at him, stared into the impenetrable dark eyes that sat deep in his head and nodded. Yes. Yes, I thought. I do believe. God help me, but I do.

"Eat with us, Horace," The Snake Stick Man offered, "a hot meal will do you good."

"Very well," I said.

Then, remembering that we had lost all our provisions during the shootout at Barradale's Camp, a question formed in my mind. "Where," I asked, "did we come across the makings of this meal?"

The Snake Stick Man smiled at me again and shook his head. "Eat of this that I provide to you, and gather strength for the journey ahead," was all he would say.

We ate in silence, the three of us sitting in the

back of the beyond, deep in the ancient Appalachian hills, shivering in the gun-blue dawn.

CHAPTER 10
BACK TO BRYSON CITY

After we finished our meal, The Snake Stick Man stood up and announced that we would call off the search for Buck Ruff and head back to Bryson City. He was sure that Buck was no longer in the area and that we should waste no more time or resources in searching for him.

I opened my mouth to, I don't know what I was going to say, exactly. Not to protest, as I did not care if we found Buck or not, and not to bother speaking of the law because I was now quite sure this journey had nothing to do with earthly justice at all. So I was unsure what I was going to say and yet felt compelled to speak, but Catch put his hand on my arm and shook his head, "no."

So I said nothing.

We walked halfway across the mountain that day and spent the night in the home of a reluctantly hospitable man named Tuckett. His house was warm, but the pallets he made up for us on which we slept were crawling with fleas.

We came across a logging road the next morning and hitched a ride into Bryson City on a farmer's hay truck that just happened to be passing by.

All in all, the trip home was remarkably uneventful. Barely a word was spoken between us the entire journey. But my thoughts were racing along with my pulse. I could not wait to get Catch alone, away from The Snake Stick Man. There was something I had to say to him.

CHAPTER 11
WAYS THAT ARE DARK

Once we returned to Bryson City, life went on in a remarkably conventional way. Within a few days The Snake Stick Man left town, headed off to another case somewhere back out west after receiving a telegram from his employers at the US Marshal Service. I returned to my rooms at the boarding house, and Catch returned to the bosom of his family at their home on the Cherokee Reservation, behind the Qualla Boundary.

As you know, dear reader, I had grown very close with Catch's family and felt them to be a replacement of sorts for the one I had once had and lost when my wife and child left me. So you may imagine my concern for them all when we returned to Bryson City without our quarry and, therefore, without Catch's five hundred dollars in bail money.

Even though Catch's family had their patriarch returned to them miraculously uninjured, they still did not have the money they needed to survive. You see, the economic calamity that was still to come, the market crash of 1929 and the misery of the Great Depression was still somewhere over the horizon for most of America. But in the wilds of Appalachia, where Catch and I lived, depressed prices for farm goods following the end of the Great War had taken an already impoverished rural population and exposed them to the pain and deprivation of the impending economic collapse years before the rest of the nation.

Many people in Appalachia were already poor and close to starvation in 1922. Following our unfruitful raid into the Sugarlands, Catch and I found we were not far behind them.

After a shared supper on one of the many evenings I spent at Catch's home, I stepped outside to light my pipe. I did not smoke inside the house as Catch's wife and son had a great sensitivity to tobacco smoke. We had dined that evening on venison shot in the woods nearby, potatoes grown in Catch's garden, and a wild apple cobbler made with sugar bought by the very last of the money I had left over from the sale of my most recent book. Everything had been scrounged, and nothing save the sugar was store bought. We had hardly anything left at all to sustain ourselves.

Catch stepped out onto the porch next to me and rolled a cigarette. As you know, he only ever smoked when in the most terrible distress, and as I lit a match for him, I could see pain and fear reflected in his eyes.

We had not spoken of the strange events of our raid into the Sugarlands with The Snake Stick Man since we returned home except for one time. I had broached the subject, concerned for the state of my friend's soul following what I now had come to believe was a pact, if not with the Devil himself, then with some lesser demon of no less danger. But Catch was adamant. He did not believe that anything of any sort of supernatural nature had occurred.

"But you, Catch," I had said, "You saw things with your own eyes. Experienced miraculous events with your own body. You felt the lead tear into your belly and then felt it healed the very next day. How can you not believe?"

Yet it mattered not. There was no convincing my friend of the truth of his recovery, no matter what I said. And furthermore, his anger at being reminded of it caused him to keep me at a distance for some time. It was a most painful thing for me to endure, the loss of my friend and surrogate family over what was only my truest and deepest concern for them.

So when, late the following winter, Catch once again invited me to his home, I leapt at the chance to visit with the friends I loved so much and missed so dearly. And it was following this meal and happy reunion that I found myself outside on the porch with Catch.

He took a deep breath and expelled the smoke from his lungs. It hung in the still night air, catching moonlight.

"I'm ruined, Kephart," he said. "There is no money left. I got no work. If we had gotten ahold of that damned Buck Ruff last year, I could survive on the money we got turning him in. But we didn't, so there ain't any, and I am desperate."

"Yes," I agreed, "I, too, am ruined. There is no money left, and I have been unable to find any work myself."

We stood there in silence for a moment longer. I knew what Catch was about to suggest, and I was already forming my answer.

Finally, Catch offered up his plan. "I have just enough left to buy some copper line. Do you have enough to buy some corn?"

I nodded.

Catch and I were about to embark on the very same business adventure that had drawn the Law down on Buck Ruff. We were to become Moonshiners.

There are two types of Moonshiner. The big-time man and the little moonshiner. Big-time men are not much better than common gangsters who run their businesses like the mafia.

The little moonshiner is a more interesting character, if for no other reason than that he fights fair, according to his code, and singlehanded against tremendous odds. He is innocent of graft. There is nothing between him and the whole power of the Federal Government except his own wits and a well-worn Winchester or muzzle-loader. Although a criminal in the eyes of the law, he is soundly convinced that the law is unjust and that he is only exercising his natural rights. Such a man suffers none of the moral degradation that comes from violating his conscience; his self-respect is whole. And it was that type of Moonshiner that we became.

It takes three men to run a still, two if you hustle, and being unwilling to split our profits a third way, Catch and I resolved to take turns that winter in the isolated log shanty where we hid our clandestine work. One of us minded the still while the other made runs to town in a borrowed vehicle in order to buy supplies and make deliveries.

The still was located up high in the mountains, far from prying eyes, but near a source of running water. You need a constant supply of fresh running water to make 'shine, and our shanty was hastily constructed in a small clearing near a diminutive mountain stream. Once the 'shine was made and bottled up, we took it down to a holler in the valley below and left it in a shed. From there, we took it by pickup to various buyers in the local towns.

The way down the mountain road from the holler where we stored our finished product was treacherous, and there was a blind curve at the end of Grayson's Gap that took many a driver by surprise, local and out of towner alike. I feel I may have mentioned this blind curve to you before. In any case, it was there that I managed to lose a full load of corn liquor once when driving too fast. I skidded off the road and turned our truck over on its side.

Catch was angry about the lost moonshine as well as the cost of repairing the truck but was relieved I had not died. He made me promise to take it slow on the back roads from then on. And take them slow, I did. Unless, of course, I was being followed. Or thought I was being followed. So Catch relieved me of my duties as a delivery driver, taking them over himself, and stationed me, permanently, at the still in the woods up on the mountain.

And so one night, when I was alone in the shanty while Catch took his turn as the delivery man, a blizzard come up and snowed me in. I was sitting by the still, minding the fire and the mash, and listening to the wind blow when I heard it. A far-off howl.

I knew what it was at once. And when I heard the footsteps approaching the door of the shack, I knew it was coming to visit me. So, at once and without resisting—

KNOCK, KNOCK, KNOCK!

—I opened the door.

There he was, Buck Ruff, the Wolf Man of Appalachia. The Black Dog of South Mountain.

He was only half beast now, transforming enough to cover himself with fur as a defense against the cold but not changing completely.

I could yet see the man beneath the monster as it stepped through the door and into my moonshine shanty.

"What do you want?" I asked.

"Betrayed me, Kephart. Done made a fool a' me," he answered. "I asked you just after Barradale's Camp. I coulda kilt you. Torn you to shreds. But I didn't. Instead, I asked you to help me. Told you to let Catch die. But you didn't, did you, Kephart? Didn't let him die. You was too slow to find him, and you let him live. And now he will suffer, same as me."

"Suffer how?" I demanded. "What will you do to him?"

"Me?" The Wolf Man growled, "I ain't gonna do nothin'. It's The Snake Stick Man that's gonna take him. And soon."

I did not understand and told Buck as much.

Buck, The Wolf Man, explained to me then that

he had once run across The Snake Stick Man years ago when he was a young moonshiner. Buck had been mortally wounded in a backwoods firefight between himself and a few Revenue Men. As Buck had crawled across the ground, bleeding to death, The Snake Stick Man had appeared to him. Just as with Catch in the cave, the Shadow had danced, and The Snake Stick Man had made a deal with Buck. His soul for his life. And Buck, fool that he was, had agreed.

But Buck's life after The Snake Stick Man healed him had been but a half life. Because, just as the Granny Woman had told me, at night, when The Snake Stick Man called to him, Buck turned into a monstrous beast and was forced to do The Snake Stick Man's bidding. It was a fate so terrible that Buck, not known to anyone as anything resembling an empathetic man, grew to hate the horrid things he was compelled to do because of how they harmed the people around him. So he tried to resist the call of The Snake Stick Man, tried to resist his commands. He found that it was difficult, but not impossible, to disobey. And the further away from The Snake Stick Man that Buck was, the easier resisting his will could be.

There were limits, however, like when The Snake Stick Man's life was in danger during the shootout at Barradale's Lumber Camp. The Snake Stick Man had commanded Buck to come to his aid and aid him he had.

Bullets do not kill the Black Dog of South Mountain. They do not harm the Wolf Man of Appalachia. In fact, what I had once read in Dahlgren's book I had also seen with my own eyes. The more lead one fires into the Wolf Man of Appalachia, the larger and stronger it becomes.

It was after this raid on Barradale's Camp, when The Snake Stick Man had Catch in the cave, that Buck realized The Snake Stick Man planned to make the same deal for Catch's soul that he had made for Buck's. And as I said, although Buck was not an empathetic man, he wished no one to suffer the same fate he had. So, unable to resist The Snake Stick Man's power with him so close, he had tried to enlist me to save Catch's soul. He hoped to have me disrupt the evil ritual in the cave long enough to allow Catch to die before The Snake Stick Man could buy his soul. That is what he had meant when he stood over me in the woods outside Barradale's camp and said, "Help."

But the call of The Snake Stick Man became too strong, and Buck had to leave me for a time before explaining the situation. And my leg was so badly injured, my strength so sapped, that I passed out before Buck could return and explain things. So he took me to his Grandmother, the Granny Woman, and asked her to heal me and explain the truth in time for me to stop

The Snake Stick Man from trading for Catch's soul.

But Catch was dying too quickly, and my leg healing too slowly, even with the help from the Granny Woman's magic, to make it to the cave in time.

So, Catch did trade his soul to keep his mortal life. Even if he did not remember it that way.

Truth be told, even had I understood what Buck was trying to tell me back then when he stood over me, transformed into the Wolf Man, I think I would not have had the strength to follow through and let Catch die. I am weak when it comes to the ones I love. Catch was the closest thing to family I had anymore, and I could not stand the thought of a loneliness so profound as the loss of my best friend.

I do not think I could have let him die if I had known there was a way to save him, no matter the consequences.

"Why, Buck? Why have you come to tell me this now?" I asked.

The Wolf Man shuddered and shook the melting snow off his back the way a wolf or a dog shakes to do the same.

"Because, Kephart. Time is comin' for your friend Catch. And I can't bear to be the reason another man suffers this fate, my mis'rable fate. Ol' Snake Stick only keeps one of us at a time. Only needs one Wolf Man at a whack. And when he makes a new deal on a new soul, he takes a gander in the book, and it tells him when that new soul is fixin' to die.

"And when that new soul dies, 'Ol Snake Stick is there, waitin' on its everlastin' spirit. And when he takes of it in his evil hands, I am released of this, my burden. No longer will I be the Black Dog of South Mountain, and I will finally allowed to die. But that new soul, the soul of'n your friend the Cherokee, he becomes what I am now. And damned he will be. Damned to walk this earth as the Black Dog, as the Wolf Man of Appalachia, murderin' and killin' on the evil Snake Stick Man's command, until either Gabriel sees fit to blow his horn and end this godforsaken Earthly mess, or The Snake Stick Man sees fit to take him a new soul."

"What do I do?" I asked, for I was at a total loss. "How do I stop this?"

Buck sat back on his hairy, canid haunches and pulled his lips back into a snarl.

"You die, Horace. You die to rescue your friend's soul."

Buck was almost entirely transformed into the Wolf Man now, his ears and mouth growing pointed and long, his eyes falling deeper into his furry brown. I thought perhaps he was going to take me to hell right there, right then, but he made no move against me.

"It's tonight when Catch is set to give up the

ghost. On the likker run to town, in that damn pickup truck you flipped before. The Revenue Men are on to him. They done set a trap and are waitin' on him out on the road to town. Ol' Catch is gonna make a run for it. But while he's speedin' down the road through Grayson's Gap, he'll hit a patch of ice and crash him the truck. And when he dies in the wreck, Ol' Snake Stick is gonna be there, a' waitin' in the trees to take his soul to hell and make his body evil. Evil like mine is now."

You may think I would be skeptical of all this talk of souls and hell and Gabriel's horn. But I must tell you, my conversion to faith, my belief in powers both good and evil, was carved on my heart ever since I saw the Wolf Man tearing through the bodies of those outlaw lumbermen at Barradale's Camp.

I was convinced of the truth of Buck's words.

Still unsure how to stop The Snake Stick Man from taking Catch's soul, I said as much. The Wolf Man became angry and stood up, the hair on his back raised up like a rabid dog's. "Like my grandma told you before the Shadow took her yonder to the flames. Trick him, Kephart! Don't let Catch take the truck. You drive it and Catch lives. Then the deal is broken!"

The Snake Stick Man must have been closer than we realized because Buck soon lost control of himself and began to snarl and snap his teeth at me.

"Maybe I'll kill you now, Kephart," he growled, "and jes' let your friend take my place."

I ran from the moonshine shack out into the cold night and leapt across the creek. The Wolf Man paced on the other side of the bank, rage in its eyes and murder in its howl.

How lucky for me that just then, I had remembered a passage from Dahlgren's book, *South Mountain Magic*. I remembered that the Black Dog of South Mountain could not cross water, and that may have given me just enough time.

CHAPTER 12
WORD OF GOD. LAW OF NATURE.

I ran. Heart racing and lungs burning, I ran through drifted snow and barreled down the mountainside.

I could hear the Wolf Man's howls heading north, making for the start of the creek, a place high up the mountain where water sprang forth from between two stones. Once there, he could cross the creek without crossing water by climbing above its rocky genesis and come for me.

Tree branches and icy wind cut my face and tore at my exposed skin. I had left the shanty in such a hurry that I did not bring my winter coat with me.

I made for the valley, running directly for that particular holler where we stored our moonshine. We had a strict rule: never, ever approach the hidden holler in a straight line, especially when there is snow on the ground, but I had no choice. Time was of the essence, and the Wolf Man was making up ground quickly.

Besides, it did not matter if our hiding spot was found. This was the last run. No more moonshine, no more Snake Stick Man, no more nothing, for me anyway.

I do not know if you have ever attempted to travel through mountain snow afoot, but if you have not, let me assure you, it is agony. The hard, icy top of the drifts crack beneath you, and your legs drop down into a quicksand of soft white powder, draining you of your strength and sapping you of your energies.

As I strode through this white hell on two legs, I was acutely aware of the Wolf Man's four-legged advantage, and I redoubled my efforts. I became so winded the thought crossed my mind that I may die.

No!

No, I thought to myself. You will not die now. Not yet. When your friend is safe in the bosom of his family, then perhaps, but not yet. For I had made up my mind. The Wolf Man was correct. If not for me, Catch would never have gone on the Raid into the Sugarlands after Buck Ruff, and he would never have been made to deal with the sinister Snake Stick Man. The agony of the Great War should have been more than enough to earn my dear friend a few years of peace with his wife and son. But no. I had ruined that.

I had ruined everything.

My own family had abandoned me years before

for reasons that are quite understandable. I was a difficult man. An unpleasant man. I had allowed the worst parts of me to poison the best thing that ever had come into my world.

I would not allow that to happen again.

Forgiveness, forgiveness, I thought to myself as I struggled to descend that frozen, winter-white mountainside. I had seen evil. Therefore, I was confident its opposite must exist. So God would forgive me, I hoped, for what I was about to do.

Heavy breathing and thundering step announced my presence long before my silhouette was visible in the blue moonlight. Catch was waiting in the Holler, crouched behind our old Ford, cigarette in his mouth, drawn gun in his hand. The truck was loaded and ready to go, the engine's rumbling muffled by the thick snowfall, vapor rising silently from the exhaust pipe.

It was a miracle Catch did not shoot me on sight. I was not expected in this secret place, and this was a moment of great danger and strain for my friend.

"What the hell are you doing here, Kephart?" he roared, finally recognizing me. "Who's watching the still?"

"No time to explain," I wheezed, my mouth dry as sandpaper, lungs screaming for air. "We are discovered."

"What?" Catch blinked and tried to comprehend.

"The Revenue Men. They know you plan to make a run down the state road tonight. They lay in wait for you now."

Catch was at first confused, then angry, then suspicious. How did I come to know the Revenue had laid a trap? How could I be sure? And why had I waited to tell him until now? I could make no good excuse and was forced to tell Catch the truth.

"The Wolf Man of Appalachia is Buck Ruff, and Buck Ruff is the Wolf Man. He was transformed by The Snake Stick Man's black magic. He came to warn me that The Snake Stick Man will make good on his deal with you this very night. He plans to take your soul at the side of the road after the Revenue make a corpse of you."

Catch did not look angry as I expected him to. He seemed mostly disappointed.

"Kephart," he moaned, "that's just superstitious bullshit. You should see a head shrinker." And with that, he made to get in the truck.

"No!" I cried as I grabbed his coat and pulled him away from the vehicle. "You must not go! The evil is real! You have seen it with your own eyes. How can you not believe?"

Catch studied me, his eyes unable to hide the pain he felt.

"I just don't. That's all."

"How is that *possible*?" I demanded. I could not imagine how a man who had seen the same things I had seen could somehow come to a different conclusion than I had.

"Because," Catch fairly screamed, "I can't! It's too much. Don't you understand? Damn you, Kephart! I was born here in the land of my ancestors, but the government, your government, tells us how we should live. I've been a soldier. I traveled across the ocean. I wore the boots. I carried the gun—"

Catch's words trailed off. He lit another cigarette, and as he did, he stared at the long, deep scars on his palms.

"I saw things over there," he breathed, "things no one should... No. Not just saw. I did things. Awful damn things, Kephart. And sure, I did them because people who have more say than me, the army, the government, they told me to. But I was the one who acted. I done them, no one else. That's on me. Then I come home to my people's home, and still, the government, that same government that sent me over there, and white folks, white folks like you, treat me like I'm some kind of second-class citizen. And then my daughter. My poor baby daughter—"

Catch's words caught in his throat. He came the closest to tears then as I ever saw him.

"The pain, Kephart," he continued, "it is enough. The horror of my real life is enough. And this Snake Stick Man and his Black Dog, this Devil and his Wolf Man, whatever you think it is, whatever the old tales say they are, I don't need it, and I don't want it. There is only this."

Catch pointed first at the ground beneath his feet, then pulled up his coat sleeve and pointed at the veins in his arms.

"The ground below me, the blood in my veins, the breath in my chest. This is all there is and all there will ever be. I can't take it if there is anything more than that."

"Oh, my dear Catch," I whispered, my voice quivering, "I am sorry."

"Yeah, yeah," Catch grumbled, flicking a bit of ash from the end of his cigarette before placing it back between his lips. "It's alright. It's alright. Look, you try to understand, Kephart. Most people don't. But you really try, and that's why—".

Catch paused there and seemed to mull something over in his mind before he continued. "You care enough to try, and that's why I call you friend. That is why I love you. So just go back up the mountain and watch our still while I make this run to town, okay?"

I nodded, deeply touched, but said nothing.

"Besides," Catch had a sideways grin on his face

as he said this, cigarette clamped between his teeth, "if there is a Hell, you know my ass is headed there anyway."

It was at that moment that we heard the Wolf Man. He was closer now.

"Forgive me," I said as I threw the punch that knocked Catch unconscious.

"My dear friend," I whispered as Catch slumped to the ground.

He may not have believed in the Wolf Man's prophecy and The Snake Stick Man's power, but I did, and there was no way in hell I was going to allow The Snake Stick Man to get his hands on my friend's soul. Not this night. Not this way. So I put the unconscious Catch in the nearby shed to keep him out of the weather, then made for the truck. I pushed in the clutch and jammed the pickup into gear.

Once inside the old Ford and roaring down the road, I came to two realizations. First, the snow was heavy here but not near as bad as at the higher elevations where the moonshine still was located, so while the roadway was treacherous, it was not impassable.

Second, I had no idea where I should go or what I should do now that Catch was safe in the holler and I was in possession of the moonshine. Perhaps, I thought, there was no need for me to die tonight. If I took the load of illicit liquor down the road away from town, then dumped it in the river, no one would be the wiser, the Revenue would not find me, Catch's deal with that Demon would still be broken, and I could go on living and spending time with my friends for who knows how long.

Suddenly, I heard the startling report of gunshots! The back windshield shattered, and the whining and roaring of truck engines and police sirens screamed out into the winter night.

I jerked the wheel to the side as a bullet entered my arm, tearing flesh and crushing bone. The truck tires screeched, and the steering wheel shuddered, but I managed to get the vehicle back under control and kept going. The Revenue were hot on my heels. They must have been watching the holler, not only the road into town. The Revenue kept shooting, and I kept driving, a mad dash into the Appalachian night toward what end I no longer knew.

Trees whipped by on the side of the mountain road. The Revenue Men kept shooting, peppering the truck with lead.

They hit one back tire.

BANG!

Then another.

But I kept driving. Motoring on with what seemed like wild abandon. But now I had a plan. My time in these hills had prepared me for a moment like this.

I made for Grayson's Gap, for on the other side was that hairpin turn on the blind curve above the cliff. I knew it was there, but I was reasonably sure the Revenue did not.

The old truck shuddered and screamed, the iron wheels sparking against stones on the gravel road. Blood poured from my wound, and I felt dizzy. Hot lead buzzed past me, exploding out of the barrels of the Revenue Men's guns and cutting a deadly path through the night air. But still, I drove on.

There it was! Just ahead was Grayson's Gap. I leaned on the throttle, picking up speed. The Revenue did as well, desperate as they were to catch me. The Gap was close now, and I made my move. I hit the brakes and cut the wheel, taking my truck toward the hillside.

As the old Ford careened into the roadside ditch, I held my breath and prayed, but there was no need to be afraid now because my plan had worked. The Revenue Men blew by me, taken completely by surprise, and flew over the side of the mountain. I heard their trucks crunching against ancient Appalachian shale as they skidded down the hill.

I could hear them yelling and cussing as they tried to get their vehicles back up onto the road, but

I knew they would have no luck, at least not until morning. The winter weather had them trapped.

I gingerly backed the old Ford out of the ditch and made my way down the road in the other direction, wholly unconcerned with the damage I was doing to it by driving on two completely flat tires.

I was alive! I had outwitted both the Revenue Men and The Snake Stick Man all in one night! Catch was alive, safe, and I was too. I could not believe my luck as I tore down the road, heading for the river to dump this load of Moonshine and making all sorts of plans for the future when —

— The Wolf Man leapt from the trees beside the road, landed on top of the truck, and broke the driver-side window with his massive paw.

He reached into the cab and grabbed my wounded shoulder, sending lightning bolts of pain up and down my body.

"Forgive me, Kephart," he growled as he jerked the steering wheel to the side and sent us careening off the road and into the trees, "I am no longer myself."

I remember little of this moment other than the smashing and screeching of the crash, followed by the dull rumble of an idling motor and spinning truck wheels. Then, I blacked out completely.

***

When I opened my eyes, I was lying on the ground,

staring up into the black night sky. Snowflakes were falling, tiny pallid dancers descending from the dark night above down to the winter white ground below.

The Snake Stick Man was kneeling over me, holding his serpentine staff.

"Am I dying?" I asked him. He smiled that strange smile of his and shook his head.

"No. Tonight is not your night. Isn't written in the book like this. Catch is supposed to be lying here in the ditch."

"That's right!" I managed to croak, a surge of happiness momentarily replacing cold dread and the numbing pain of the gunshot and the crash. "Your unholy pact is broken."

Again, The Snake Stick Man just smiled. The curve of his lips and the shine of his teeth unnerved me.

"Unholy," he mused, "those are the words of God. But I am not the word of God. I am the law. The Law of Nature, the Law of the Wilderness. And holiness makes no difference in my world. There is only give and take. Life, death. Weight and counterweight."

I blinked snow out of my eyes and spit blood. Cold dread was returning, along with the pain in my arm from the gunshot.

"But, but Catch did not die tonight."

"No, he did not," The Snake Stick Man purred,

"but one night he will. There is no escaping that. And when he does, I will be there to collect. The same goes for you, Kephart."

The Snake Stick Man stood and turned to leave.

"What about his baby daughter? What about that part of your deal?"

The Snake Stick Man stopped and turned back to face me, a silhouette of black against the white winter drifts.

"I keep my word, Kephart. She will be born again, but not for many, many years. And Catch will not know her as a living man. That was the agreement. Maybe someday when he is my new companion and has taken Buck's place as the Black Dog of South Mountain. Maybe then he will see her. But not before."

And with that, The Snake Stick Man again turned to leave.

The Wolf Man trotted up on all fours, sniffed my face, and snarled at me. Then he took his place at the Snake Stick Man's side, and they walked together in lockstep through falling snow into the ink-like gloom of the Appalachian winter night.

I could not imagine Catch ever taking Buck's place at The Snake Stick Man's side. My friend's will seemed too strong. But what did I know? Apparently, not very much.

I watched Buck and The Snake Stick Man until

they were swallowed by the darkness of the forest, and my eyes were closed from exhaustion.

***

That was the last page.

Rain and thunder battered the shop as I closed the book and turned to face the Bookseller who still stood behind me.

"Is that it? Is that all there is? What happened to them?"

But the Bookseller did not answer me. Instead, he pointed at the rising floodwaters. "We'd better go to the roof," I said. "Flood is getting worse."

He looked out the window. I was right. The water was rising and washing under the doorjamb, flooding the shop again.

Not all bad news, I thought to myself. At least that thing was gone.

We made our way to the back door, up the fire escape, and onto the rooftop. We sat together, me and the Bookseller, huddled under an awning.

"You told me there would be answers," I said, ducking raindrops and closing my coat tightly but ineffectively against the weather.

The Bookseller nodded.

"There were answers," he said.

Then he smiled again, that strange eternal smile, and as he did, the now familiar sound of the strange howl once again made its way across the hollers and hillsides.

When I heard the howl this time, I felt something stir inside me. The Bookseller noticed.

"Feel it now, don't you?"

It wasn't a question. He knew I did.

And yes. I felt it. I was thinking it. But I didn't yet believe it. I turned away from the sound of the howl and looked deep into the Bookseller's craggy features.

How old was he? I thought to myself.

"I was adopted," I blurted out, surprising myself with my own outburst. I was not sure why I started telling the Bookseller about my past, but once I started I could not stop myself.

"They found me on a firehouse doorstep," I continued. "Nobody knows who abandoned me. There was no information. Someone had written my name on a scrap of paper and left it with me. That was it."

The Bookseller cocked his head and looked into my eyes, urging me to keep going. So I did.

"But I was always curious about my heritage," I said, "Always wondered who I was. So I finally took a DNA test a few weeks ago."

"Did you, now?" the Bookseller mused. "What did the test say?"

What did I think it would say? I wondered to myself. What did I want it to say?

"The results never came back. They lost my sample in the mail," I answered.

It was the truth. I still did not know where my family was from or who they were.

The Bookseller smiled even wider this time.

"Your name. It is the same as hers." He spoke quietly but with force.

"Same as whose?" I demanded.

"She was given an old French name before they buried her, one his wife's family used often," the Bookseller continued. "It meant 'much loved.' Armandine, they called her. Like you."

"Who?" I demanded. "Who was named Armandine?"

The Bookseller took a deep breath and pursed his lips. "Catch's infant daughter. The one he and his wife lost in childbirth and buried in the garden under the dogwood tree. The child Catch bartered his soul for."

Lightning struck again, close, and temporarily blinded me. When I opened my eyes, the Bookseller was gone. I was alone on the rooftop. The storm was fading away, finally, and I stood up and looked out over the rooftops of the small town.

My name. The little girl who died and The Snake Stick Man promised to bring back. She and I had the same name.

Armandine.

There was howling again in the softening rain.

I could see it, standing on the rooftop opposite, its black fur wet and glistening from the rain, its white teeth almost glowing in the semi-darkness. But despite the intimidating size and monstrous bearing, when I saw the Wolf Man now, I was not afraid. I just watched it for a while, and it watched me with dark, sad eyes.

Then, as quickly as it had appeared, it was gone.

Eventually, the weather cleared completely, and the flood waters receded. I made my way back down the fire escape to the street below and looked for the Bookshop entrance, even though I knew it would not be there.

And I was right. It was gone, just like the Bookseller and the Wolf Man.

I wondered, did I wish to see it again? The Black Dog of South Mountain, the Wolf Man of Appalachia, or whatever name I could give to the fever dream that was either as real as me or a concoction of my mind. What would I say to it? To him? Because he could not be what I thought he was. What the Bookseller said he was.

But what if...?

Had an eternity of his pain been worth it?

I banished the thought from my mind and started walking. But as I walked, the thought came back to me, again, and again, and again, until finally, I could no longer chase it away.

An eternity of trouble.

Was I worth it? Was anyone worth that?

I think that, perhaps, is an unanswerable question, regardless of the truth or fallacy of Kephart's lost manuscript, which I still held in my hands.

The Bookseller and his shop had disappeared, but the book itself was a physical reality I could hold onto.

As I walked down Market Street, searching the wreckage of the flood for my car, I thought several times that I saw something in the shadows, something like the Wolf Man, watching me, and I would walk forward expectantly, hoping to catch one last glimpse.

But every time I turned a corner, I found nothing there but a memory.

Ryan Michael Hines is a novelist, podcaster, and screenwriter based in Los Angeles, CA, who loves the Southland sun but misses the beauty and mystery of the Appalachian Mountains every day.

A graduate of UCLA's prestigious MFA Screenwriting Program, Ryan has written several award-winning scripts. *His TV pilot EASTSIDE OUTLAWS was developed under a First Look Agreement with Sony Crackle. His feature adaptation of EASTSIDE OUTLAWS won Best Crime Feature Screenplay at the 5th LA Crime and Horror Film Festival.*

MOONSHINELAND is Ryan's debut novel and was inspired by his narrative podcast of the same name.